Disney
Better
NATE
Than Ever

Also by Tim Federle

Five, Six, Seven, Nate!

Nate Expectations

Tim Federle

SIMON & SCHUSTER BOOKS FOR YOUNG READERS
New York London Toronto Sydney New Delhi

SIMON & SCHUSTER BOOKS FOR YOUNG READERS
An imprint of Simon & Schuster Children's Publishing Division
1230 Avenue of the Americas, New York, New York 10020

For information about special discounts for bulk purchases, please contact Simon & Schuster Special
Sales at 1-866-506-1949 or business@simonandschuster.com.
The Simon & Schuster Speakers Bureau can bring authors to your live event.
For more information or to book an event, contact the Simon & Schuster Speakers Bureau
at 1-866-248-3049 or visit our website at www.simonspeakers.com.
Also available in a Simon & Schuster Books for Young Readers hardcover edition
Interior design by Laurent Linn
The text for this book was set in Minister Std.
Manufactured in the United States of America
0222 BID
This Simon & Schuster Books for Young Readers paperback edition March 2022
2 4 6 8 10 9 7 5 3 1
The Library of Congress has cataloged the hardcover edition as follows:
Federle, Tim.
Better Nate than ever / Tim Federle.—1st ed.
p. cm.
Summary: An eighth-grader who dreams of performing in a Broadway
musical concocts a plan to run away to New York and audition
for the role of Elliott in the musical version of E.T.
ISBN 978-1-4424-4689-2 (hardcover)
ISBN 978-1-4424-4690-8 (eBook)
[1. Musicals—Fiction. 2. Theater—Fiction. 3. Auditions—Fiction. 4. Broadway
(New York, N.Y.)—Fiction. 5. New York (N.Y.)—Fiction.] I. Title.
PZ7.F314Be 2013
[Fic]—dc23
2011050388
ISBN 978-1-6659-2084-1 (movie tie-in pbk)

For Rueby Wood and Aria Brooks

Disney
Better
NATE
Than Ever

Some Backstory

I'd rather not start with any backstory.

I'm too busy for that right now: planning the escape, stealing my older brother's fake ID (he's lying about his height, by the way), and strategizing high-protein snacks for an overnight voyage to the single most dangerous city on earth.

So no backstory, not yet.

Just . . . fill in the pieces. For instance, if I neglect to tell you that I'm four foot eight, feel free to picture me a few inches taller. If I also neglect to tell you that all the other boys in my grade are five foot four, and that James Madison (his actual name) is five foot *nine* and doesn't even have to mow the lawn for his allowance, you might as well just pretend I'm five foot nine too. Five foot nine with broad, slam-dunking hands and a girlfriend (in high school!) and a clear, unblemished face. Pretend I look like that, like James Madison.

I do, except exactly opposite plus a little worse.

By the way, despite our tremendous height gap, he and I weigh the same. The school nurse told me that once: "James Madison was just in, before you," she said, grinning like her news was a Christmas puppy, "and you weigh the exact same!" This is the one attribute at which I'm *not* below average: body heft.

Oh, and I already knew that James Madison was in the nurse's office before me that day, because we'd just passed in the door frame, and he licked the Ritalin crumbs from his lips and lunged at me to make me scream a little.

I screamed a little.

Luckily, I picked a good key and turned the shriek into a melody, walking into the nurse's office humming a tune. Life hasn't always been easy (my first word was "Mama," and then "The other babies are teasing me"), but at least I'm singing my way through eighth grade, pretending my whole existence is underscored.

There. There's your backstory. I was always singing.

Not that there's any evidence. My parents weren't very good about documenting my childhood; my older brother got all the video footage, including his first seven poops. By the time I was born, disturbing the tranquility of Anthony's remarkable career as a three-year-old wonder-jock, the video cameras were fully trained on his every sprint, gasp, dive, and volley.

Those are sports terms. Reportedly.

So I always sang, not that there's any proof of it. No high-res shots of little Nate Foster scurrying around the Christmas tree, belting "Santa Baby" in a clarion, silver soprano.

That's just my imagination of my voice. Again: Nobody ever recorded it.

But I'm getting off track—you're distracting me—and there is a lot to do.

"No pressure, but if you pull this off, you are going to be my hero forever." This is Libby, my best friend for as long as I can remember (two years and three months, specifically, but I hate when stories are hampered by math). Libby's standing in my backyard tonight, lit only by the moon. Although it might actually be the neighbor's motion-activated floodlight.

"Bark! Bark!" That's their dog. Yes, she's definitely being lit by their floodlight.

"Libby, if I *don't* pull this off and make it back home by tomorrow night, I'm dead. Like, my parents will never let me leave Western Pennsylvania again."

I'm hugging my bookbag, which is stuffed with three pairs of underwear, one plastic water bottle (singers have to stay hydrated), deodorant (just in case I need it on the trip; so far I'm good, but I saw on the Internet that a teenager's body can begin stinking at any moment), and fifty dollars. Fifty dollars should be safe through at least Harrisburg, and once there, I'll take my mom's ATM card out and get some more cash.

Oh, yeah. I borrowed my mom's ATM card. I'm babysitting it, we'll say.

The plan is this: If I get money in *Harrisburg*, it'll be less suspicious than visiting an ATM in our little town (unofficial motto: "48.5 miles from Pittsburgh and a thousand miles from fun"). When she gets her bank statement, Mom won't suspect it's me who stole from her; Harrisburg is the capital of Pennsylvania and thus must be crawling with big-city criminals.

"I'm serious, Lib. If anything goes wrong, my parents'll never let me leave home again. Ever."

"Luckily, they've never let you leave home *before*, either. So if you get permanently grounded for this, Nate, you won't really know what you're missing out on anyway."

Unless I get trapped in New York without a hotel, in a freak late-October blizzard. Unless I finally make it back here after my trip and really *do* know what I'm missing out on, because I actually eat one of the famous New York street pretzels. Imagine: pretzels sold on the street! It's as if anything is possible. Do they also sell hopes on the street? Do they sell hugs and dreams and height-boosting vitamins? Or hot dogs? I bet you they do.

Feather circles my feet in the grass, whining. I'm

sure he has to pee. Feather is so well trained (my older brother did the dog rearing; he's not only the town sports star but a dog whisperer, too, in addition to donating his old issues of *Men's Health* to the library and also volunteer lifeguarding) that the dog only "goes" when we instruct him to. For a moment I want to believe Feather's just sensing that I'm leaving. That he's only whining because he's scared. As scared as I am.

"*Go*, boy." But really, he just has to pee.

Something stirs in the woods behind the house. Libby crouches down and her jeans strain at the knees. We have identical bodies, other than the obvious stuff.

"So we're good on the alibi?" I say.

"Yes. We're good. I'll cover your dogsitting duties while Anthony goes off to win another track meet tomorrow. And if anyone calls your landline, I'll pick up the phone and disguise my voice as yours."

Libby's being kind. We have the exact same voice already. When I order pizza, they always sign off by saying, "That'll be thirty minutes, *ma'am*."

"Let's go over what happens if somebody tries to kidnap you," Libby says.

"I act like I'm gonna barf."

"That's right." She has theories for everything, and one of them is that if you throw up on criminals, they'll run. She watches more TV than I do.

"What if I can't barf? What if I haven't had anything to eat?"

Libby smirks, reaching into her own bag and handing me a twenty-four-pack of Entenmann's chocolate donuts. Nobody knows me like Libby.

"You're so good to me," I say. "Oh, gosh." Now I'm hopping. "Maybe I should just stay home? This is crazy."

"Don't you think it would be crazier to stay here? And sell flowers the rest of your life?" The family legacy is a floral shop, Flora's Floras. Mom runs it now, though we're not making any real money. There's nothing like a business in which your main product wilts by sundown.

"And tell me one more time," I say, "what my New York catchphrase is? It's—uh—*Gosh, that A train subway sure is running local again*. Right?"

Libby groans and takes me by the shoulders. "No, Nate. The key is to get it exactly right. *The A train is running local today, what a hassle.* That's the phrase. I Googled 'things that annoy New Yorkers,' and I need you to trust me." She twitches her nose, her habit when she's nervous or certain I'm about to screw something up.

"The A train is running local today," I say like a studious robot, "what a hassle." I can handle this.

The neighbor's floodlight clicks off, and for a moment it's just me, Libby, Feather, and a sky of rural darkness, the crisp autumn air that leads to adventure. Or trouble. A bonfire that burns too hot, or a Halloween prank gone horribly wrong, or a boy getting murdered in New York City.

"Close your eyes," Libby says. And when I do, and she *doesn't* take my hand and put a treat into it—a lucky rabbit foot, once; tickets to a tour of *Les Misérables* another time—I sense something new is about to happen.

And just as I'm opening my eyes again, and watching her coming at me like *I'm* a chocolate donut, her mouth open and eyes closed and arms reaching out to me, my brother pulls his pickup truck into the side yard, high beams on full blast. Sixteen-year-olds always drive with their high beams on, to make up for their insecurity and lack of experience manning a seven-ton death toaster.

For the first time ever, Anthony has saved me from something.

"What are you freaks *doing* out here?" he says, slamming the truck door and turning his baseball hat around backward, rolling up a sleeve like he's about to get into some dirty work.

"Keep your voice down, Anthony," I say, "the neighbors are probably sleeping."

"Oh please, Nathan," he says, circling the entire length of his truck, inspecting it for the tiniest nick (this is a ritual). "Aren't you usually belting out the chorus to *Gays and Dolls* or something around now?"

Try loving showtunes alongside an older brother who can bench-press your weight. No, literally! Before he became too embarrassed to be seen in public with me (right around when Libby dyed my hair blond), Anthony would bench-press me out back and we'd charge seventy cents to the neighborhood kids if they wanted to watch.

"It's *GUYS and Dolls*," I'm about to say, but don't.

Libby moves away and looks at the stars, probably horrified that she was about to kiss me and got interrupted. Probably horrified that she was about to kiss me at all. "We're hanging out here because there's supposed to be a meteor shower tonight," she says, lying to Anthony. I'm the only person she doesn't lie to. "And your little brother and I never miss a show."

I'm sweating so bad that I think this might be the first time I actually need deodorant.

"Listen," Anthony says, walking over to us but stopping a full eight feet away, like we're going to infect him with terminal jazz hands or something, "I've got a huge meet tomorrow, in Aliquippa. And I have to be up at the crack of butt. So if you're planning on staying up all night playing your theater games, howling at the moon, you might as well sleep at Libby's. I'm serious. I've got to get my rest, Nate."

Perfect. He's playing right into the plan.

"Well, gee, Anthony, if this game is such a big deal, maybe that's a sensible idea."

"It's not a game. It's a *meet*."

He makes for the broken sliding screen door (years ago, Anthony wrestled me through the kitchen and out onto the back patio, smashing through the screen, ending up grounded for the first/last time in his whole flawless life) and disappears within, reemerging a moment later. "And don't do anything stupid tonight, guys. I'm serious. Mom and Dad will kill me if they have to ID your body at the morgue."

Anthony is supposed to be watching me this weekend, though I don't know what parents, in their right minds, leave their gentle-souled thirteen-year-old in the charge of their girl-crazed sixteen-year-old.

This is not to say my parents are in their right minds.

Only that they're broke. Only that they can't afford a babysitter, let alone the special weekend Dad is treating Mom to, on account of their admittedly remarkable seventeen years together. I think Dad was just too cheap to afford a divorce, so he splurged on a fancy hotel, someplace that probably has terry-cloth robes and heart-shaped good-night chocolates.

Someplace parents like mine will renew their vows and think life can always feel this refreshed, from this anniversary night forward. Until they get home tomorrow and find that their younger son went missing in New York City.

Mood killer!

And now, with Anthony and Feather inside, and Libby and me alone, there's nothing left to do but leave.

"I'm scared, Libby," I say, choosing to pretend the almost-kiss never happened.

"Why?" Libby says, but I can see she's scared for me, too. Or wishing she could come. Wishing she could be the co-adventurer in the fantasy she lit in the first place, introducing me to the magical escape of musical comedy. "There's nothing to be scared of, Nate. You're small and scrappy and can get out of any situation the world throws at you."

Just this past week, I'd been stuffed into a locker by a seventh-grade nose picker who is shorter than I am.

"Okay, your Lyft to the bus station is supposed to get here in, like, ten minutes," Libby says, walking me to my own fence. "I told him to come to the bottom of the hill, so Anthony wouldn't see you bailing." What would I do without Libby? What *will* I do?

"What if I make a schmuck out of myself? What if I forget the words to my song?"

"You've been making a schmuck out of yourself for years, Nate," Libby says. "At least this time you've got the possibility of being paid for it."

"What if I stutter my name?" I always stutter my name: N-n-nate F-f-oster. Like I'm confessing to the crime of being alive.

"Let go and let God," Libby says, "or whatever."

"What if I lose my voice? What if—"

"Nate, just stop." She snaps her fingers. In my face. "You're going to sleep on the bus and arrive at nine in the morning. You're going to ask any adult who doesn't look like a murderer which way it is to Ripley-Grier studios, and you're going to find a bathroom and splash down your face and try to run the hot water long enough that it steams any wrinkles out from your shirt, and you're going to be fine." She looks me up and down. "Do you have cough drops?"

"Yes."

"Do you have your water bottle?"

"Definitely. Duh."

"Do you have your headshot and résumé?"

"Holy *Dance of the Vampires*, no! *Dance of the Vampires*!" (Instead of cursing, we shout out the titles of legendary Broadway flops. *Dance of the Vampires* was an infamous musical from the early two-thousands, starring the original *Phantom of the Opera* actor, this time as a blood drinker. Evidently it featured an entire song called "Garlic." Not even kidding.)

"Okay, okay, let's not panic," Libby says. I must've left my headshot and résumé at her place, last night, when this entire adventure scheme was hatched. "It could potentially be very charming to Broadway," she reasons, "discovering a boy from off the street who doesn't even have a photo of himself. Besides, let's be honest about your résumé: You've only played a mushroom in a junior high pageant about the merits of eating vegetables."

She has a point. Although I played the broccoli.

Also, I don't really even have a headshot, so Libby and I just took my eighth-grade picture and blew it up, revealing my horrible skin and overuse of hair product and that blasted underbite that I always forget I have. This is one of the reasons I'm actually not so sad my parents didn't document my life. This is one of the reasons I'm glad I left that picture at Libby's last night.

The Lyft pulls up, and she hands me a fifty-dollar bill.

"Libby!"

"Just take it. Your dad might be a doctor, but it's not like he shares the wealth." My dad is not, in fact, a doctor. He is a maintenance engineer at the University of Pittsburgh Medical Center—he cleans toilets—but whenever classmates hear my dad works at the Medical Center, they just assume he's a doctor, and who am I to ruin another kid's dream?

"I'll pay you back," I say. "With interest. I'll make this up to you."

She looks around, checking for stray raccoons on the frighteningly dark back road to my house, and sticks out her index finger at me. I do the same, and we touch them and smile, and she says, "Don't forget to phone home, yeah?"

"Definitely. I'm just going to be gone for a day. I'll be back by this time tomorrow night."

"You better be. Your brother and parents will be pulling in at the same time, and you know he's going to have a pickup truck full of trophies, and they're gonna be ready to kill each other. And there's something very, like, *specific* about arriving home and realizing your thirteen-year-old is missing. Even if they never notice you when you're—you know—*here*."

"You getting in, or what?" the driver calls out from an open window.

I look at my outfit, like maybe I'm actually dressed as SuperBoy and can just avoid this cab ride altogether. Like maybe I could just *fly* to New York and avoid getting mugged in the Greyhound bathroom before I even make it out of Pittsburgh.

"Break a leg," Libby says, hugging me and giving me a quick kiss on the cheek. "And text constantly, and here"—she thrusts a mysterious manila envelope out at me, pulled from her bag. "Take this, and don't open it till after your audition. After they fall completely in love with you."

"Thank you, Libby. I will." And they won't.

And from just above, a star blasts a trail across the night sky—like a visor of fire on Libby's head—leaving it glowing a finger-painted smear, something human and touchable and reachable. Like maybe I could make the same kind of mark in New York, somewhere that might actually understand me.

Maybe Libby wasn't lying about the meteor shower after all, or can sense things about the future that even I can't.

"Get right back on the bus, after the audition," she says. "Don't go to the wax museum in Times Square or anything. Buy me an 'I Heart New York' T-shirt and then just get here. Just get back here."

I shut the door and roll down the window. The car smells like a dead person, what a dead person might smell like if ever I'd smelled one. I'm sure I will on this trip, if I don't end up one myself.

"Libby?"

"Yes, Nate?"

"If anything happens, you were always my favorite Elphaba."

The cab skids away, and I hold my bag close and shut my eyes and say a frantic prayer that it all goes off okay. And when I turn around to wave to Libby, she isn't there—just that streak across the sky, still glowing.

Burnt into the Big Dipper like a dare.

Theories on Everything

For the record, I now know why they're called Greyhound Bus Stations, and it's not what you think.

They lure you in with the promise of a sweet, fast dog with a cartoon rib cage, but you should just drop the "hound" part of the Greyhound Bus equation. It's all about "grey." Everything here is a different color of grey. The hair of the homeless people, even the young ones: grey. The lighting: grey. The hot dogs: grey (but actually pretty tasty). Everything is the color of death, of a foggy day that promises another D-minus on your History homework.

Everything is the color of a wilted flower from my mom's shop.

God, she'd kill me if she knew I was here.

"And how much is a round-trip ticket to New York City, please?" I say at the counter. I am up on my tiptoes, trying to appear a mildly short boy and not a medically tiny alien child.

"Round-trip," the guy says, looking half-asleep or perhaps dead; looking grey, "is a hundred dollars."

"A hundred dollars?" I say, losing my balance and knocking a bunch of Greyhound pamphlets to the floor.

"Yes, a hundred dollars. Or fifty-five one way. But your mom or dad don't have to pay in cash. We accept credit cards."

"Funny you should ask about my mom, sir," I shout. "I figured you might do that, figured this might be the first thing you bring up when somebody as little as me—as little *looking* as me—walks up to your Greyhound ticket counter, a counter you're doing one heck of a job manning, to request a ticket out of here." I'm losing him. I'm losing him. "It's downright ludicrous, I'll admit as much, but on the topic of my mom: She's just in the bathroom. And I'm sure she'll be out in just a moment, but she's going through a bit of a stomach ailment and asked that I please take care of my ticket, alone, before she gets out. Because it could take quite a while."

Libby and I had rehearsed this speech, and perhaps even over-rehearsed it.

"You know stomach ailments, sir," I say, attempting an off-the-cuff improv.

"You need to be fifteen years old to purchase your own ticket," the man says, looking above at a TV monitor of the local news. Somebody was just stabbed three blocks from here, which comes as a strange comfort: Perhaps New York will be safer than Pittsburgh.

I pull Anthony's ID from my wallet, swallow hard, and slide it across the counter. If this man takes an even vaguely close look at this picture—the headshot of an international model, a brother who could be anything in the world he wants (though he's lying about his height; he is *not* five foot ten)—I'm dead.

Thank goodness the coverage on the local dog-napping is so dynamic that the man is riveted, not looking away, taking Mom's ATM card from my hand and going to swipe it when I stop him.

"Wait!" I say, pulling the card away. "I need to pay this in cash."

Just what I'd need: a credit card statement arriving for Mom that says ILLEGAL PURCHASE OF NEW YORK CITY GREYHOUND TICKET BY YOUR UNDERAGE SON.

Luckily, I caught him in time.

Luckily, Libby and I prepared for this.

We worked out every covert detail of my trip, yesterday, when she showed up at my house after school. Picture it: I was pretending to rake leaves in the backyard, in actuality smack-dab in the middle of my signature, chore-avoiding *Singin' in the Rain* routine (it was pouring out). Libby arrived, panting, breaking the news about the audition in the first place. I get all my headlines from Libby.

And news she had: "Jordan Rylance"—the lucky twerp across town who goes to the Performing Arts School—"announced a very special trip he's taking to New York City, Nate," Libby said, grinning like a Lotto winner. "To audition for a Broadway musical version of *E.T.*, called *E.T.: The Broadway Musical Version*." (At that point, I grabbed on to Feather's tail, for balance.) "And they're looking for a young boy to play Elliott. And there's an open call in Manhattan, this weekend."

And Libby squatted and shielded her face, knowing how I always react to world-shaking news. Knowing I would launch anything on my physical person—coins; old friendship bracelets; the rake—thirty feet in every direction, like a supernova star explosion.

Knowing this was my one-shot ticket out of Jankburg, Pennsylvania.

And now, *almost* using my mom's ATM card only twenty minutes into the adventure, I wonder how I could have managed the nerve to think I might pull this off.

I step away from the counter and fish through dollars from my plastic bag full of money, and when I return to pay, the sleepy man has been replaced by a woman who has the same non-look on her face as he did, but with more makeup.

"Can I help you?" She is eating potato chips and they look delicious, by the way.

"Oh, the gentleman before you was helping me, was all set to let the transaction go through." Cool down, Nate. "But—uh—I figured you might do that, figured this might be the first thing you bring up when somebody as little as me—as little *looking* as me—walks up to your Greyhound ticket counter, a counter you're doing one heck of a job manning, to request a ticket out of here. It's downright ludicrous, I'll admit as much, but on the topic of my mom: She's just in the bathroom." Shut up, Nate. Shut up, Nate. "And I'm sure she'll be out in just a moment, but she's going through a bit of a stomach ailment and asked that I please take care of my ticket, alone, before she gets out. Because it could take quite a while."

The lady continues to eat potato chips. "Okay," she says, not asking for Anthony's ID or anything, selling me one ticket.

One ticket to my dreams.

Which costs fifty-five dollars not including tax, these days.

And now I'm staring out the window at a familiar world zooming past, colors bleeding from grey (Pittsburgh) to bright red and blue (a car accident) to brown (somewhere thirty minutes outside of town). Libby shared a really good technique that is thus far working beautifully: Crumple up a bunch of Kleenex and put them on the seat next to yours, and nobody will sit next to you on long bus trips. Try it sometime, guys.

I practice my smile.

From the time we leave the rest stop and make it to Harrisburg, capital of Pennsylvania and crawling with criminals, I practice smiling in the face of fear. *Anything* could happen at this audition. I could forget my words; I could stutter my own name. But if my smile is firmly intact, if I can show that I'd be an ideal employee, someone who'd never cause a problem, maybe they'll hire me just for the team spirit I'd bring. Twelve minutes into the smiling exercise, my jaw cramps. Underbites are not designed to be overworked or tested.

I have two donuts, for comfort.

A woman in front of me is listening to something loud on her headphones, trendy music that Anthony probably knows, and that would *normally* irritate me—but tonight, the distraction is pulling me out of my own terrified, self-doubting mind. Her head bops to the downbeat, hair cascading up and over her seat into my lap, and I wonder if New Yorkers have such big hair. Probably not. They probably all shave their heads or have discovered some other trend that is going to be totally intimidating and exciting.

What if I have to get a temporary tattoo at the border, as we're pulling in to New York Manhattan City Island? What if they stamp my hand like at the underage club Anthony goes to on weekends, and what if the ink is so dark on my pale, lifeless, grey-Jankburg hands that my mom immediately recognizes it: the stamp of a bad kid who snuck away.

She'd kill me.

No, she actually would. "Don't try to run away from home or anything stupid. I'll kill you if you get yourself killed."

Actual recent quote.

Okay, I didn't want to do this, but take a two-minute detour with me. You need to meet my mother. It's time.

A Quick but Notable Conversation with Mom, a Week Ago

I had both dogs on their leashes (Feather, of course, and Mom's awful lap warmer, Tippy). We were breaking the front door when Mom appeared next to me, in her big blue parka. Uh-oh.

"Lemme just walk you to the corner," she said, "and you can take them the rest of the way down past the Kruehlers'."

Often when I'm walking Feather (alone), I pretend I am Don Quixote and he is my faithful sidekick, and we go down to the creek behind the Kruehlers' house and I sing "The Impossible Dream" at the top of my little lungs. You're not going to believe me, but I've had newts stop and stare.

Before Mom and I'd even gotten out of the front yard last week, she blurted, "So, Daddy is taking me away for the weekend."

"You're kidding!" I said, stepping on Tippy (which

is somehow short for Tiffany), who yelped like a sticky faucet.

"Yes, first time in seventeen years," Mom said, with not a whole lot of enthusiasm. Feather spotted something in a bush and got low, his tail parallel to the grass.

"So where are you guys going?"

"The Greenbrier. The Greenbrier in West Virginia. It's very fancy and expensive."

Silence. Who knew birds could even chirp so loudly, *that* was the type of silence they cut through.

"Dad can afford 'expensive'?" I said, and she glared at me.

"You only celebrate your seventeen-year anniversary once, so, I dunno. I'm not going to question your father."

"Well. I'm glad for you two."

"Thanks," she said, probably happy that someone was endorsing it. Probably worried—as worried as I was—that they couldn't afford such an extravagance.

She broke away to take Tippy home, to let me walk Feather the rest of the way around the block, and turned back to say, "Don't get into any trouble around the neighborhood, Nate."

"Sure thing, Ma."

"The Kruehlers called last week, to say they heard something wild howling in the woods."

Oh no.

"They thought a rabid beaver or something was in their yard, Nate, stuck in a bear trap. And it turns out Mr. Kruehler went to the lookout in their attic and saw *you* in their woods, wailing like an animal, with no regard for nature. And just prancing around like—you know."

(Like a fairy, right, Mom?)

"It's just—you have to be careful, Nathan."

I remember it now. I was acting out a scene from *Hairspray*, with Feather turning in a surprisingly believable performance as Tracy Turnblad.

"People hunt back there, Nate. I don't . . ."

"Don't worry about an accident, Mom. Anybody shooting Nate Foster would know exactly what they were aiming at," I wanted to say, but I just went, "Okay."

"Same thing at school. You could at least *try* to take a page from Anthony's book. To fit in."

Mom gets a lot of calls from school, where my only good subjects are Creative Writing and Getting Taunted. Take infamous bullies James Madison and his Bills of Rights (that's two boys named Bill, around whom James Madison specifically created a gang, because of the admittedly clever constitutional tie-in thing). They can't let a day go by without putting me through the wringer. Most recently, they cornered me after school in the gym and told me I couldn't leave the basketball court until I made "three three-pointers in a row." I asked if I could just make "one nine-pointer and be done with it," and little Bill laughed and said, "He's not unfunny for a gay kid."

(My sexuality, by the way, is off-topic and unrelated. I am undecided. I am a freshman at the College of Sexuality and I have undecided my major, and frankly don't want to declare anything other than "Hey, *jerks*, I'm thirteen, leave me alone. Macaroni and cheese is still my favorite food—how would I know who I want to kiss?")

"Are those boys still calling you Natey the Lady at school?" Mom said, her face tired and long.

"No way, Ma."

"Well, that's all, then," Mom said, scooping Tippy up and letting her lick Mom's mouth, which gives me the heebs. "Oh, and Nate. Try to keep it down around Anthony, too. He gets very religious-like about his meets, and there's a big one coming up," and she was off, back up the hill. "And he's in charge while we're away," she yelled, not even turning to face me. "Don't try to run away from home or anything stupid! I'll kill you if you get yourself killed."

See, I told you it was a direct quote.

That's all you need to know about that.

This'll Be Fast: You Might as Well Meet Dad, Too

"I hear you're taking Mom away for an anniversary weekend?"

"Your brother's in charge while we're away." Dad was doing something with WD-40 and a fishing pole. "It's important to treat a girl proper every now and then, son."

"I'll keep that in mind."

"You meeting any nice girls at school?"

"Dad, I'm thirteen."

"Can't start too young."

That's all you need to know about that.

"Met your mother when I was your age."

I *said* that's all you need to know about that.

"I'm prayin' for you, boy."

Seventy-Seven Miles to Manhattan

But forget my parents.

(Do it *for* me. Since I can't seem to.)

With the Greyhound wheels thumping a trance, I close my eyes and nod off, imagining what it'll be like in New York when I arrive. In my mind, Kristin Chenoweth will be waiting for us on a staircase at this Port Authority place, probably singing the theme to "New York, New York." And then someone'll hand out cans of Mace and tell us, "Good luck, and have the time of your life if you can keep it."

Somewhere in the middle of New Jersey, a collection of drool has pooled so impressively onto my shirt that a child in another row wakes me with his phone's camera flash. It doesn't bother me, though; people are already taking my photo and I haven't even arrived at my dream destination.

And when the blur in my eyes finally vanishes, I

see it, sticking up like a hitchhiker's thumb.

The Empire State Building.

Where I bet you need a shot of oxygen by about the thirtieth floor.

By the time we're spinning through the Lincoln Tunnel, a woman across the aisle has caught sight of my face, of my open jaw and flitting eyebrows, and calls over, "You'll never forget it. You'll never forget the first time," and I turn away and whisper to the window, "You don't have to say that twice."

And we arrive at Port Authority.

And I am lifted into the terminal.

(It's annoying to say it like that, but I'm reporting in with hard facts and was raised a partial-Christian and thus can't lie about things like hard facts.)

I and my belongings are lifted into Port Authority Bus Terminal.

I'm actually holding my bookbag so tight, it probably looks like an extension of my shirt. Or like I have a horribly distended belly, like an abscess, and have ventured to New York for surgery at one of their world-famous belly abscess hospitals.

There is such a rush into Port Authority, exiting the bus and then mazing through a series of escalators, that all I have to do is lean just slightly back and the crowd literally surges me along. This must be what it feels like when you're my brother and you score a goal and the team carries you across the field.

And, okay, if you don't follow sports references (Hi, friend!), it's like this: You know when Dorothy finally makes it to Oz? It's all just like that but less emerald tinted, and I don't see any horses changing colors yet. But hey, I'm still indoors. And besides, it's Manhattan City and I think anything's possible at this point.

I peek down, just in case I'm in ruby slippers. Nope. Nikes.

But still.

A giant lobby clock hangs above the scattered people, the crowds scramming either *to* something or away from it—I can't tell. Whatever *it* is, it's either really awesome or freaking monstrous, that's how these folks are running. 9:09 a.m. Okay. I've got almost an hour before the audition sign-up starts. I should figure out where it is, and change my shirt, and get an orange juice or something.

(No Kristin Chenoweth here, by the way, or free cans of Mace. Bummer times two.)

To exit onto the street, I point my Nikes toward the sunniest doorway and lean back, lifted by the locals. I spill out the doors like surf at the edge of an ocean (I've never been to one, but a lot of movies have ocean shots). And I feel like that, like water disappearing into the sand. It would be so easy to disappear here. Maybe it would even be wonderful.

I glance at the Greyhound bus schedule I grabbed in Pittsburgh. I need to be back on the bus by 1:00 p.m. if I hope to make it home tonight without having to tell too huge a lie. So far, I'm good: no hand stamp at the border, and nobody's tried to kill me.

The horizon, you're wondering? The look of the horizon? The horizon *isn't*. The horizon is a mile of blinking buildings. The horizon is a million adults zooming past me, is a line of yellow taxis, is more than you could possibly imagine. Just across the street is the New York Times building, a towering sheet of metal, and—my God, it's like nirvana—to my left, an Applebee's.

The biggest of its kind.

Like a super Applebee's, the Cadillac of Applebee's, an Americana food emporium made automatically bigger and better by being here. This can be my home base today. If I get lost: "Point me to the Applebee's," I'll say, real cool. "Point me to the biggest Applebee's in the world, where I bet they serve two fajitas when you order one; where I bet the shrimp fajita isn't any more expensive than the chicken."

Because I can already tell: Things are more fair here, just because everything's so fast that who'd have the time to stop and gouge a customer?

Libby said the audition would be nearby. I check Google Maps on my phone, but it's confusing.

"Are you lost?" somebody asks, and when I look up from the map, he seems just like my dad but probably with a better job.

"I don't know if I'm lost or not," I say, and realize it's the first time I've spoken since the Greyhound Station in Pittsburgh. My voice pulls on itself. "I'm looking for the Ripley-Grier Audition Studios."

"What's that?" the guy says, craning his neck to look at my phone. "Have you been to New York before?"

"Only a million times in my dreams," I'm about to say, but don't. "No."

"Little young to be alone."

I love these people already. Nobody would be so rude as to say that in Jankburg. They'd just talk behind your back. I can already tell that everything here is going to be straightforward and conditional, and I like that. It's just like me. The only thing I'm unconditional about is dessert, and how much I love Feather and musicals.

"Yes, I'm traveling solo," I say, "but I'm older than I look," and I almost launch into my monologue about Mom in the bathroom but then remember this guy isn't a Greyhound employee.

"Okay, well, from the look of this map, you want to make a right." He starts talking slowly, like I'm a tourist, which is insulting. It's our first fight, this guy and me. "We're on Eiiiighth Avenue now, and you want to walk down to Thiiiiirty-sixth Street, which is siiiiix blocks from here. It looks like it's going to be on the ooooother side of the street."

Like I'm Tippy the idiotic throw-pillow dog.

"Okay, cool. Six blocks'll take me, like, a half hour to walk or something?"

"It should take you, like, ten minutes. And there's a one-dollar pizza place on the way. And it *tastes* like one-dollar pizza, but, you know."

"It's only one dollar," I say.

"Exactly. Good luck, kid," and he leans back and gets swept up in the surge, his head bopping along, off in the direction of something called a Duane Reade.

Okay, this is it. I'm off to my first audition.

Full disclosure: If you knew how scared I was, if you saw me shaking right now, white as no cloud that ever flies over Jankburg's dreary hills, you'd know I didn't want to let on. That everything is riding on me making this happen. That I have to return home as good as Anthony is, at something. Anything. Or not return home at all, preferably.

En route, I'll get three dollars' worth of pizza, fifty cents' worth of pop—no, water: I don't want to burp at my first audition—and use my remaining cash to buy Libby an 'I Heart New York' T-shirt, and *me* a Statue of Liberty keychain and a show poster of *Wicked*, if they sell those anywhere. They must. Gosh, *Wicked* is, like, half the reason for New York to even exist.

And crossing the street (walking south, which is called "downtown," according to studies), I'm feeling good: clean underwear, twenty remaining emergency donuts, and my mom's ATM card.

What else could a guy need?

Suddenly the hordes cut in half, ducking into abandoned phone booths (there's no other kind these days, I guess) or beneath the overhang of yet *another* Duane Reade. And then I'm the only guy standing here, out in the open street.

The only guy not in on the weather forecast.

The only guy getting soaked, re-baptized a New Yorker.

The only guy grinning.

One-Dollar Pizza/Priceless Stories for My Grandchildren

I shouldn't have worn my audition outfit on the bus; that's the first big lesson.

Pack a big enough bag for backup clothes and not just backup donuts (this is nothing against the donut industry, of which I am one of the chief supporters).

But here I am, sopping wet, like I've just deboarded the log flume at the Kennywood amusement park back home in West Mifflin. Like I've never heard of checking the weather or traveling with a poncho.

To be fair, the only other time I've left the greater Jankburg area was as a tag-along with my parents at Anthony's biggest tri-state area game. Yes, a trip to Akron, Ohio, can feel intoxicatingly foreign—sophisticated, even—in that "anything that's different from me is exotic" kind of way. Also, one time, when I was a kid, we went to Orlando for a long weekend, but Mom ate a bad piece of fish at Magic

Kingdom and we ended up coming home early.

Back to New York, though. My bangs have melted into my eyes, my Nikes are drenched, and I'm shivering in the brown jacket that barely keeps me warm on mini-walks with Feather. Now it's the only thing protecting me from the harsh city elements. A cab skids past me, spraying an additional forty gallons of puddle water onto my pants—the only things, so far, that had remained relatively dry.

Great.

I have another donut.

And then, just like that, the rain lets up.

When I reach the other side of the street, finally broken from my trance of vacation nightmare stories, a man wearing a metal sandwich board—$3 SHOES + $2 HATS—thrusts a pamphlet into my face.

"Thank you so much, sir," I say, thrilled at the amount of instant friendship that can be attained here. "A three-dollar pair of shoes. Could this be true?" I crazy-shake my head, taking a cue from Feather after a bath.

"Don't know, boss," the man says, spinning on himself to propel additional flyers into the hands of the rushing masses, none of whom appear to be stopping. These people don't know what they're *missing*, that's for sure. Maybe I've landed in New York as an angel of reason.

"Where are these three-dollar shoes and two-dollar hats, sir?"

He continues his twirl. "You look on sheet," he says. "It's on sheet."

I look down as instructed (I don't think we're going to be friends, after all) and see, photocopied across the top: "39th and 8th—One Day Blo-Out Sale—Montego's Discount Warehouse."

Montego's!

"Which way exactly are these Thirty-ninth and Eighth roads?"

He stops what he's doing, dropping his arms so that the metal sandwich board pops with cheap exasperation, and groans at me. His eyes shift back and forth too quickly, set to some warp speed that would probably make me throw up if I tried it.

This could be a handy technique if I get mugged and need to puke: eye shifting.

He points downtown at a building just past the cheap pizza place: Montego's Discount Warehouse, advertising its tremendous deals with a waving plastic banner. Imagine a three-dollar shoe in Jankburg, PA! You couldn't. Everything back home has to be imported, purchased somewhere cooler. But not here, where for five dollars you can get a slice, a pair of Keds, and a new ball cap or something. I'll have to launch an investigation.

This seems like a good time to text Libby, and I look at my phone and see that she's written a billion times already, that I could have been keeping a comforting travel dialogue going. Not that I wanted to eat up the battery. Her texts range from an old-fashioned *42nd Street* reference—"go get em peggy sawyer"—to a general shout—"HAVE YOU BEEN KILLED????"—to the most recent, clocking in only ten minutes ago—"ok a bit of news here. dont hate me."

Uh-oh.

It's almost nine thirty, a half hour away from the audition sign-up, and I press call to connect to Libby, but immediately my phone powers down. It needs about seventeen hours of charge for seventeen *minutes* of chat. And PS: It used to be Anthony's before he got a *Droid*.

"I would like three slices, please, sir," I say, mall-walking into the pizza joint. And then, realizing I forgot to get extra cash out in Harrisburg (busy on the lookout for child-murderers), and knowing I'll need my money to stretch long enough to buy a dry new pair of audition shoes at Montego's: "Make that *two* slices," I say to the pizza man. "For two dollars, as advertised."

A moment later—everything happens in a moment here; I've had to wait for nothing but the rain to pass, and I can't really blame New York for its own weather—the gentleman slides two paper-thin wisps of pizza to me on a flimsy plate. I take out my plastic cash bag and pay him one dollar and four quarters.

"Anything to drink?" he says.

"No, thank you," I say, tapping on my water bottle, "I'm all good in the hydration department." Shut up, Nate.

A woman behind me asks me for spare change. Libby's on a real kick about karma these days, so I decide to be extremely selfless.

"Do you have change for a five?" I say to the lady.

"No change, man," she says. And I don't hate being called "man." That's a first.

I hand her the five and start to hoof it over to Montego's, with time before the audition all but running out. But then something truly remarkable happens.

Three teenage boys pass me, all a little taller than I am (duh) and each wearing extravagant fashions, their hair daring and swoopy; one's dancing across his forehead and another's spiked to the skies, probably able to predict the weather before the news, even.

These are the types of boys back home, maybe a year older than I am, who make it their primary interest in life to torment me.

On instinct, I push myself against the wall outside Montego's Discount Warehouse, knocking my head into the bricks (so they don't have to, I suppose), and drop my bookbag. Like maybe the tallest one—the James Madison of the bunch, though he doesn't have James's joke of a moustache—might just pick it up and steal something out of the front pocket.

But he doesn't do anything like this.

In fact, these three boys, these three kings, all cooler than anyone I've ever breathed the same air as, walk right past me. And in the best possible sense, they take no note of me at all.

Me, "N-n-nate F-f-foster," with wrists so thin I can't even wear a watch. With ankles so big I have to wear men's socks.

With an allowance of fifteen dollars a *month* for mowing the lawn every week. With clothes so dated, these three New York teenagers would probably have a poster of me on their apartment walls, as a model of what *not* to wear.

Or better yet, while all us Pennsylvania kids are doing projects on cave drawings, on early civilizations and their silly woolly mammoth skirts and dinners of forest berries, these three New York boys probably just do reports on *me*. On *my* dinners of Kraft macaroni & cheese; on my weak wrists and tubular ankles. Of Kmart slacks that these boys wouldn't even use to wipe their butts. I'd be their version of a caveman, of a guy so undeveloped, so confused by fast objects, that I'd probably get killed in my first winter without thermal underwear.

But they don't seem to care at all.

Not about me.

They're so focused on whatever joke they're telling each other that they don't have any time to mock me.

Me, with scraggly Midwestern bangs down to his soft Midwestern chin. With more holes in my ear than the ozone layer, from the time I made Libby play Rizzo opposite my Sandy (the ear-piercing scene) during a method-acting basement scene-study of *Grease*; me, with an old cross around my neck, worn to keep Mom calm. A cross that's practically burning a hole into my clavicle for all the sins simmering in my stupid head.

For the things I'd like to say to these boys to thank them for not noticing me.

Especially the tall one.

I pull away from the wall and watch the boys disappear into the crowd across the street. And then, picking my bookbag back up, I officially decide that when I'm old enough, I'm going to move here. And someday I'm going to find this tall kid and thank him, face to face, boy to boy, guy to guy.

And as I walk into Montego's—its overhead fluorescents bouncing something awful; its music pounding a calypso thump; its floor littered with tossed-off shoes—I decide I've never felt any more at home than

I have today, in this city that whizzes past me.

In this city that, brilliantly, couldn't care less about me.

"You," a guy says, an employee in a pair of jeans so baggy I could actually spend the night in them and have spare room to make S'mores, should the audition run long. "You buying anything or what?" He produces a pair of black high-tops with a purple tongue, something even Anthony wouldn't attempt to pull off. "You ready to step up your fashion?"

And I put my bag down and say, "Let me see how much money I've got in my plastic bag," and know that I'm going to leave Montego's as cool as those three New York boys. Or as cool looking at least, especially if Montego's has a barber in the back.

I know I'm going to arrive at my first audition literally changed for the better.

Definitely Changed, "For the Better" Undecide

Overall it is impossible to tell, with my fashion experience (wearing whatever Boy's Husky clothes my mom throws on the bed, once every two years), whether the new look is an improvement on the old look. The old look being the way I've looked, every day, for the last thirteen years.

Gosh, I can't believe I'm thirteen. Such an unlucky number.

My new friend Duane helps me out with the Montego's purchases (the many Duane *Reades*, he informs me, sell everything in the world: baby wipes, *Star* magazine, carrots—everything).

"Do you think I look like a ten-year-old who lives in California and rides magical flying bicycles?" I say to Duane, not kidding.

"For sure, brother," he says.

"Okay, thanks. Because"—I lift up the giant plaid Eckō Unlimited shirt he's dressed me in, something Anthony could probably catch a gust with and sail to Saturn on, winning awards and creating a new Galactic sports event—"I'm not so sure I can pull this ensemble off."

"Trust me," Duane says, texting somebody, probably a girl who likes guys in big shirts, "this is an upgrade."

I guess he's got a point. No matter how out of place I may feel, it's better to walk into a job interview dry. Wet clothes worn to a Broadway audition are probably a sign of some kind.

"Okay," I say. "And the hat?" He puts a very neato Yankees cap on me and twists it sideways, and I go to bend the brim and remove the flashy silver sticker, but Duane actually smacks my hand and goes, "Brother, the hat is fly. The hat is you." Still texting, still looking away.

"So, I should pay for all this," I say, following him to a cash register, where a young girl is smacking bubble gum and filing her nails.

(She's supernice, by the way, and even gives me a free plastic bag in which to store my original, dripping outfit.)

Back out the door, the sun is set to full blast, lighting the streets a shimmering slick. It's ten to ten, and

I *need* to get to the Ripley-Grier Studios, now just a block away.

• Bookbag: check.
• Libby's mystery manila envelope: check; damp, but check.
• Old clothes, the old me, bunched up in plastic bag, stuffed into bookbag (had to throw out one clean pair of underwear to make room, but must be smart about space): check.
• Dead phone: check.
• Most important, all remaining donuts intact: check.

I scan the addresses from across the street, walking past a comfortingly familiar White Castle, and then cross with a clump of folks who don't seem to be minding the Walk/Don't Walk signs at all. I love it here: the *people* rule the traffic, and cars must stop and—oh, wait, that Honda almost killed that lady. Okay. I've still got things to learn.

And here it is.

Ripley-Grier!

Huh.

Different than I'd imagined in my bus ride mind-movie of the day to come. Ripley-Grier appears to just be an office building, just a simple office building. The kind that other kids' dads, the ones with real jobs, would probably work in and make their families a lot of money.

I walk through a shiny-floored lobby, aware suddenly of how slippery and cumbersome my new purple Adidas high-tops are, and step up to a security guard. Here goes literally everything.

"I am here for *E.T.: The Broadway Musical Version*, sir." My voice is jittery, or I am.

"Which floor?"

"Which *floor*?" I repeat back at him. "The floor with *E.T.: The* flipping *Broadway Musical Version* on it," I want to say.

"Yes. Which floor y'visiting?" Perhaps he is being hostile with me because of my outfit.

"Oh, the Ripley-Grier Studios floor, sir."

"Sixteenth Floor. Smile for the camera," and he takes my photo. Wait: Is he taking my . . . headshot?

And this is the moment I realize the surrounding lobby is awash with a million other boys, all of whom look just like me but in clothes that fit them and are defined by primary colors and stripes. Things regular kids actually wear, and not anything like the tarp I've got on. "Anyone want to go camping," I think to call out. "You provide the kerosene and I've got the sleeping arrangements all worked out."

I board the elevator and press 16, crushed into the corner by a group of kids and their moms getting on behind me.

"Let me see your teeth," one of the moms barks to her son, a boy whose hair is parted so aggressively, I could probably see his thoughts if I stared into it hard enough. He bares his gums, revealing perfect, peppermint-Orbit-white teeth, and his mom licks both her thumbs and smooths back his eyebrows.

"What do you say if they ask how old you are?" she says to him, a little softer.

He smiles those peppermint-Orbit-white nightmares and says, "However old you need the character Elliott to be."

And I realize this audition is going to be a harder game than I'd anticipated.

Black and White to Color

The doors part, and suddenly the relative quiet of a small enclosed box is broken by what sounds like a circus, an actual three-ring circus with popcorn sellers and scar-faced boys and women who ride elephants without seat belts, such is the tremendous noise.

It's like no place I've ever been in Pittsburgh.

It's the kind of place I'd actually pay money to come and just people watch, back home. If some future Noah decides to include every stripe of person on his ark, and not just zebras and whatnot, he'd do a good job popping by this elevator exit ramp and loading up a few of these weirdos.

A blazing TV monitor announces what's happening in which studios: *Gypsy* in Studio F; *Phantom* in Studio C; *Carousel* auditions in Studio J. It's . . . incredible.

Wait: *Phantom*'s still running? Whoa.

Not that I need a room number to know where I'm heading; it's clear all us kids are here for the same reason, and just like at Port Authority, I lean back and get swept along to the *E.T.* studio.

And I see him.

Jordan Rylance.

Libby's ex-friend. From when she went to the Performing Arts School with him, in downtown Pittsburgh, before her mom got sick and they had to move back to Jankburg. Before Libby helped me learn everything I know about life and love and lozenges.

Here he is.

As I round the corner, past a Vitamin Water dispenser and a series of small practice rooms, Jordan Rylance is sitting in a chair, a perfect binder of music placed perfectly on his perfect lap. At first I think he's severely underdressed, that I wasn't the only idiot who showed up looking like one today. But then I recognize his genius move, something I'd never've thought of.

He's in a red hoodie.

Just like Elliott in the movie. And jeans more normal than mine, and sneakers that look like Hollywood sneakers playing the *part* of sneakers: perfect bowlaces and perfect white edges and perfect uncreased tongues. And he doesn't look wet at all, like he avoided the last hour's rain entirely. Jordan probably has parents who paid for a hotel next door, a hotel with a connecting walkway that led him directly to the audition.

"Mommy," I watch him whisper, waving a thermos in the air, "my water isn't hot anymore."

His Mommy jumps up, dropping a weird leopard-print coat behind (presumably to mark the territory as her own), racing away with Jordan's water canister. I fumble for my own bottle and take a sip.

It's time to get hydrated and get serious.

"Do I know you?" Jordan says, and I realize I'm staring at him, that my wide-eyed scanning of the last hour has finally met an audience who is looking back.

"Oh sorry, I—"

Twin girls bump past me, and I turn to survey a Broadway audition studio teeming with a grab bag of children. Many of the girls are practicing their splits, and a boy is posed on a skateboard, and two *other* boys are juggling balls back and forth.

"Do we have to *juggle* for this audition?" I say to Jordan suddenly. What am I doing here?

His Mommy returns, holding that boiling thermos of Jordan-water, and snaps to me: "Can I help you?" But not in an "I *want* to help you" way, like, at all.

"Oh, I was just"—I straighten up and drop my bookbag, by now pulling my shoulder into an ache—

"wondering if we had to juggle for this audition. Or do the splits. I just see a lot of kids—"

"Well, Jordan is on vocal rest," his Mommy says, squeezing a packet of honey, pulled from her purse, into his water. There appear to be several lemons, as well, in that purse, and a whole mess of lozenges.

I've got lozenges too, I think to myself, and I don't even have to deal with an overbearing mom.

"What's vocal rest?" I say, and Jordan pipes up, breaking some rule I'm sure, and says, "I'm sorry, do we know you?"

"Well, you're Jordan Rylance, right? I'm N-n-nate F-f-foster"—pull it together, Nate—"and I go to General Thomas Junior High, across town, and—"

The very mention of my lower-income school makes Mrs. Rylance go white, like I'd robbed their house or poisoned their poodle (they're *so* obviously the type of family with a poodle, probably named Killer or something cutesy).

"Well, it's nice to meet you," Jordan says, reaching out his hand. I shake it, and when he pulls away, his mother—her eyes still locked on me—unsnaps a keychain-Purell and vigorously douses Jordan in it, practically giving him an entire hospital bath.

"Jordan, baby," she says. "Shh. Save it for the audition." She brightens her face. Artificially. "So, what are *you* singing, *Nate*?"

"Oh, gosh, probably 'Bigger Isn't Better' from the Broadway musical *Barnum*."

"I love that song," Jordan says. "I used to sing that song when I was a kid."

His mother stands up and says to me, like I was caught teasing Killer the poodle, "Okay! Have you signed in yet? You should sign in, because they're very backlogged and we wouldn't want you to miss your spot," and literally turns me around and gives me a teeny shove toward a young woman behind a table in the far corner of the hallway.

"I'll see you later, Jordan," I call back, pushing through the canopy of children—what if there were a fire or something?—into my place in line.

I see the important young blonde woman behind the check-in table talking to the mother of the girls who bumped past me before. "Are they twins?" the blonde woman says. "They're so cute." And their mom has the nerve to say, "Are you *looking* for twins for the play?" and the young woman says, "Oh, I don't know, I'm just an assistant in the casting office."

There is so much to be confused about here.

A small tree, something that looks native to the palm family, sprouts from behind the woman, distracting me further: Do palm trees grow in New York? Is this a land where anything is possible, even tropical indoor plants? And are girls even *allowed* at an audition for the character Elliott?

When I finally reach the front of the sign-up line, the juggling brothers have tossed a ball into a framed show poster of *Chitty Chitty Bang Bang*, and it crashes to the floor, scattering glass everywhere. The non-twin girls shriek, and the blonde casting assistant woman leaps up, and maybe I should just go. Maybe this is a perfect moment to pick up my bookbag and march back to Port Authority and just write the whole endeavor off as an exploration of New York City and nothing more. A scouting mission toward a future trip.

"Hi, there," the casting assistant woman says. Oh my gosh, it's my turn. Her face is shiny and warm, but dotted with those same warp-speed darting eyes all the people here have. It's like everyone in New York is afraid they're going to be caught cheating at poker. "Are you here for the audition?"

"Yes. And I can't believe the A train is running local today," I say, trying out Libby's catchphrase on my first adult.

"Okay," the casting woman says, laughing, handing me a clipboard and a pen. For a moment I think she's asking for my autograph, and I panic, wondering which signature I'll use: the one with all lowercase letters that connect, so the *e* of Nate loops into the *f* of Foster; or the one where I sign it like a cross, Nate going left to right, Foster coming down on the page like a crossword. Sharing the *e* for Foster, I mean. Not to be complicated.

But it's just a form that she's handing me, like at a dental office. And that never goes well for me.

"I'll just need you to fill out this sheet, and have your mom or dad or guardian sign it. Assuming," she says, tapping my hand with a pen like we're best friends studying for a test, "you're under eighteen." She winks.

"Sure, sure," I say. But then I start sweating straight through my billowy new shirt, and could probably use an official moment alone with my deodorant. *Mom or Dad or a guardian's signature*. This is a disaster. After pulling off one of the great suburban escapes of all time, I'm getting sidelined on a technicality. (It's like at the Olympics, when after a million years of training, some high diver accidentally has a poppy-seed muffin and can't compete because his pee test looks like he's had drugs or whatever. Anthony told me about this phenomenon once, when he was beating me up.)

I retreat to a small hallway alcove, imagining backup scenarios. I could ask perfect Jordan Rylance's mom to cover for me, to sign as my guardian. But *she* would probably take the opportunity to pull a matchbook from her purse (in addition to lemons and honey, I'm sure she carries matches). She'd light my application on fire, cackling like a mad witch. Maybe I'll go as her for Halloween.

Who are you dressed as? Libby would say, still trying to cheer me up from this disastrous New York mission that will end as well as my family's trip to Magic Kingdom did. *Some kind of suburban housewife?* I'd be in a Mrs. Rylance wig and would turn to Libby and say, *A suburban house witch, actually, who drives her son to auditions and then burns the other boys' applications.* My costume would be her horrible wig-hair and a purse full of fruits and matches, and honey packets, and a general demeanor of bloodthirsty competition.

Okay, so I won't ask Mrs. Rylance to cover for me.

The audition application is otherwise so simple, taking care of my lost résumé and everything. I wonder if I can list Libby as an acting teacher: We've drilled my *Brighton Beach Memoirs* scene-work so deep into the ground, I could practically do a one-man tour of it, dripping in found oil.

Not that I'm old enough to play the part of Eugene. I'm never old enough for anything.

And that's when I get the idea. The best idea ever.

NAME: Anthony Foster

AGE: 21

HEIGHT: four foot eight (it's genetic)

WEIGHT: not sure, happy to stand on scale or call doctor back home; need phone charger if the latter is necessary

RELEVANT PROFESSIONAL EXPERIENCE:
I played a piece of broccoli and understudied the legumes in a local pre-professional production of "Vegetables: Just Do It."

YEARS OF VOCAL TRAINING, AND TEACHER: 2 years and 3 months, teacher: Libby Ann Jones

DANCE TRAINING? 2 years and 3 months, Libby Ann Jones

ACTING TRAINING? 2 years and 3 months, Libby Ann Jones

STUDIO: ____________________

Studio?

"Excuse me," I say to a very pretty girl in a wool skirt. "Do you know what this means? 'Studio'? On the audition application form?"

She shakes her head, and I see that she's polishing a flute.

Is anyone *else* here just a regular schlub from the back roads of Pennsylvania, dressed as a hip-hop artist, who not only *doesn't* play a flute, or juggle, but sometimes has a hard time keeping his balance tying his shoes if he's had too much dessert?

"'*Studio*' just means the dance studio you attend," a guy says, an uncle type with a helpful vibe. "For instance," he continues, and I see that he's in some kind of jazz sneaker, "I run a performing arts studio in Florida, for gifted children. Like my nephew, Shawn."

Shawn appears from behind his uncle, dressed in the identical outfit (pleated khakis; pleated hair; pleated Polo).

"And so Shawn would list my studio, the Robert Poppins School of Performing Arts, under that column on the application. Shawn, tell this boy how many pirouette turns you can do."

"Eighteen in tap shoes," Shawn says, with one strange, lazy eye distracting me, "and six in jazz flats."

"But he did *nine* in jazz flats at the competition in Virginia Beach, didn't you Shawn?"

"Well, technically I spun on my heel. I did most of the turn on my heel and not full relevé. Not on my toes like you coached me to, Uncle Robert."

Uncle Robert shakes his head at Shawn and says, "Not if they ask, you didn't, Shawn. If they ask in the audition, you take the average of both your turns—eighteen in tap shoes and nine in flats—and you just tell them you're able to do thirteen at a moment's notice."

"What if they ask me at that very moment, when I'm done auditioning?" Shawn is eyeing a big wooden door where we must be going to get judged. "What if I get in there and they ask me to do thirteen pirouettes?" He appears as nervous as me, which is amazing, since he can do an average of thirteen pirouettes, no matter the shoe, and I wasn't even sure what a pirouette *was* all these years. Every time Libby mentioned it, in passing, I thought she was mentioning a special kind of pastry that Broadway people ate in the green room before going onstage.

"They won't ask you that, Shawn," Uncle Robert says, his fake-red hair glowing something purple in the wash of sun streaming through a far window, "because they wouldn't want to intimidate the other children at the first round of auditions. And I can't imagine 'Elliott' has to do thirteen pirouettes, anyway. It's *E.T.*, for crying out loud, not *Firebird*." Uncle Robert directs his attention to me. "A lot of people don't realize that children at a studio like mine can already perform more difficult tricks than many, many Broadway professionals can. Even adults. Isn't that right, Shawn?"

But Shawn's lazy eye has reached its limit, dropping entirely to the bottom of his socket, and he nods off for a second and then pops his head up, disoriented, beginning the whole trick again. Uncle Robert hands him a PowerBar.

That wooden door from across the hall opens, and a man—just bursting with life, with long flowy hair and a long flowy shirt and a long flowy face—walks up to the blonde assistant woman with the shiny face, and they whisper. She stands and claps her hands, not in a fun cheerleader way but like she's already mad at all of us for something.

"Listen up, please," she says, and the hallway is instantly quiet. I watch Mrs. Rylance cross her legs and pat Jordan on the knee, and he's smiling so hard

I think he actually splits a corner of his mouth open. "We are about to see the first fifty children," casting assistant woman continues, "and the cutoff today is three hundred. Please look at your application, if you haven't turned it in, and make note of your number."

Number ninety-one.

"We will take in fifty children at a time, and do a type-out"—this makes Uncle Robert groan—"and it will take approximately twenty minutes, per fifty kids." All this math, it's harder than algebra. I thought the very *point* of New York was that there was no homework, only dangerous subway rides and Brooklyn Bridges and giant-size Applebee's. And *Wicked*.

"So," the casting woman continues, "this could be quite a long day, and I encourage everyone to make use of the snack shop down the hall, or to get outside and get some fresh air."

A mom with a hoarse voice raises her hand and wails, "Is the director in there?"

"I have a creative team list, here," the casting woman says, really shouting, actually, "of the adults in the room today. But when your children go in for the type-out, they will be introduced in person." She sits back down, and the hallway descends into a panicked demiroar.

"What's a type-out?" I say to Uncle Robert.

"It's where they line you all up," Robert starts.

"Like you're a criminal, accused of stealing cookies," Nephew Shawn says, stupid Nephew Shawn who actually thinks stealing cookies is a crime. Maybe it *is* in Florida. Who knows. They have alligators in pools there, so anything's possible.

"They line you up and decide," Uncle Robert says, "simply upon your looks and type, whether you are even appropriate to *sing* for them. To advance to the *actual* audition portion. It's ridiculous and very old-school." He takes out a swatch of knitting and bounces his leg. "When I lived here in the nineties, it was all the rage: You'd audition for Jerry Mitchell and you couldn't even get through the door without them practically throwing boiling water at you." Uncle Robert's lips have gone frothy white, spittle forming.

Also, I had no idea men were allowed to knit.

I lean back in my chair. So I guess an "audition type-out" is a lot like gym class, where student captains are chosen (never me) and one at a time you're picked for their team (never me).

"Silence, please!" the blonde casting assistant screams, bellowing over the buzz of mothers putting makeup on their girls; of boys singing scales; of every other child nervously retucking-in his or her shirt. (For some reason, when people are very nervous, they untuck and retuck their shirts.) "Please return your application as soon as possible, because I have to get the team lunch."

The *team*. What does that even mean?

Back to the application.

STUDIO: Robert Poppins School of Performing Arts

It's a minor lie, a white one, and looking up at Uncle Robert, I can tell—his hair is *just* this fake-shade-of-red enough—that he isn't a big enough deal in the dance world for anyone to cross-reference my fib. This Uncle Robert guy doesn't know anyone on Broadway, I can just sense it.

HAVE YOU EVER SEEN THE MOVIE E.T.?

Yes, it is my favorite movie.

(It is, too, not lying.)

WHAT'S YOUR FAVORITE PART IN THE MOVIE, AND WHAT DO YOU CONNECT TO MOST IN THE STORY?

Oh, Lord, this is like psychology. This is the kind of thing people in Jankburg make fun of, the kind of flamboyant stuff that got the arts funding all but cut from my school in the first placc. *The only thing children should be connecting to*, my dad would say, *is each other, in a football uniform. Or connecting to a blasted* scholarship. *I'd like Nathan to connect to a nice pre-med scholarship before he ups and connects to a flipping movie about a bunch of kids and their pet alien friend.*

WHAT'S YOUR FAVORITE PART IN THE MOVIE, AND WHAT DO YOU CONNECT TO MOST IN THE STORY?

I liked how the dad was never around.

WHAT IS YOUR AUDITION SONG TODAY: "Bigger Isn't Better" from the Broadway musical Barnum

HOMETOWN: ____________

I think on this one. They're probably looking for Broadway-savvy people who won't get lost on subways and be late for rehearsals. But I decide on a seven-lie limit for this application, and calling myself twenty-one probably counts as four. I wish Anthony's fake ID weren't such a stretch. I could probably pull off eighteen, blaming it on a condition, some shrinking-boy thing, but twenty-one . . . I dunno.

HOMETOWN: Jankburg, Pennsylvania

IF YOU ARE HIRED FOR E.T., AND AREN'T FROM NEW YORK, WOULD YOU BE WILLING TO RELOCATE TO NEW YORK CITY? If I don't get hired for E.T., I'd be willing to relocate to New York City.

ARE YOU A MEMBER OF ANY ACTORS' UNIONS? ____________

I pause.

"An actors' union," Uncle Robert says, and I realize he's looking over my shoulder, "is what professional actors belong to, with years of authentic training and time spent in the trenches trying their hardest to make it." The froth is back on his lips. "So you can put *no*, you're not a member of any actors' unions."

"Okay." Union*s,* plural. There are multiple. Wow. Probably separate unions altogether for child jugglers and people who can do the splits.

"And then," he continues, "you can erase my performing arts studio as a reference. Unless," and Uncle Robert stands and clears aside a horrible little hallway throw rug, "you'd like to get up and have a pirouette competition with my nephew Shawn, right here. And if you can beat *him*, by all means." The girl with the flute is staring at us now, having finished the polishing business and begun nibbling celery. "If you can beat my Shawn, I'd love to claim you as a student."

Nephew Shawn does a knee bend and cricks his neck from side to side, like he's done this a billion times. If a pirouette actually *were* a pastry, I'd be delighted to have a pirouette competition with Shawn. I could out-eat anyone here, I bet you.

"No, thank you," I say, the crowd of auditioning onlookers moaning in disappointment, "I don't want to twist my knee in these new Adidas." I wave them for everyone and erase Robert Poppins School of

Performing Arts from the application, feeling a total moron. "Sorry about that, Professor Poppins."

"Okay!" the flowy man from before sing-songs, shocking me out of my embarrassment, forcing a scratched line across the whole audition form. "We want the first fifty kids, lined up single file outside this door. And, moms! That means you have to put away your iPads and your purses and your *own* dreams!" This gets a tremendous roar from all the moms. "And clear this aisle so your kid can be the next big thing. But listen!" Everything is exclamation points with this guy. "We only want kids who really, *really* want to be here, who go to bed at night and dream of Broadway and wake up in the morning and cry for Broadway! Who eat, bathe, and juggle Broadway." Here, he pats one of the juggling boys on the head, like he already knows him from Juggling Union membership meetings. "So please, please, only line up if you and you *alone* want to be here, kiddos!"

All the kiddos, everyone but me, who is horrified at this clown, jump up and down like he's handing out chocolate-covered cotton candy, and Uncle Robert takes Shawn's hand and starts toward the lineup.

"Where are you going?" I say, and Uncle Robert turns back and sneers, "We were here at dawn. Shawn is in the first group," and I go back to my application and finish up.

SPECIAL SKILLS: Lying on applications, I'd love to write, debating further entries: Stealing brother's ID; Wearing inappropriate clothes to auditions, and finally, Great admirer of children who can do multiple pirouettes. But I decide to be simple and honest.

SPECIAL SKILLS: I thought a pirouette was a pastry, before this audition, and if that's any indication of how much I could learn in New York, I hope I have a chance to live here.

I take the form to the casting assistant woman and slide it over facedown, hoping she won't look too closely.

"Okay, Anthony," she says, "thank you very much." She takes a pen and writes "#91" on a name tag, the sort of thing my dad might wear to the company Christmas party, once a year when the janitors are actually allowed to mingle with the heart surgeons. "Just put this number on your shirt," she says, "and think about taking off your hat for the audition."

My Yankees cap, its unbroken brim hovering over my forehead, had become totally forgotten, another thing that isn't really me. Another foreign object in a day full of them.

"Wait," she says, squinting at the application. Oh, *Carrie*!! She's discovered the lie.

(*Carrie*, a nineteen-eighties megaflop musical,

was based on the Stephen King novel of the same name, and evidently featured a mile of Spandex and fake pig's blood, and wasn't even played as a comedy.)

Carrie!

"Anthony?" she says. "Didn't you mean to put *twelve* for your age? Because the numbers are reversed, here—it says 'twenty-one'—and I think that might not be true." She picks up a tremendously huge Starbucks drink and sips at it and is *acting* like she cares, but her eyes are still darting that already-recognizable Manhattan Dart.

"No. I mean yes. I wrote twenty-one."

"Okay." Her arm is shaking under the sheer weight of mocha. "Are you here by yourself?"

"Well, look *around*, there's hundreds of us," I think to say, but don't, managing just, "Uh."

She takes my application off the clipboard, folding it directly in half, writing a red *X*—suddenly she has the biggest red Magic Marker I may've ever seen, bigger even than her Starbucks—and drops my form into a garbage can below the desk. A garbage can that I swear wasn't even there a second ago. I have a knack for spotting garbage cans, because I so often end up in them, headfirst.

The hallway is quiet, as still as that horrible elevator ride, and all fifty of these children, lined up against the wall, are gaping directly at me; so are the other million, with their moms and dads and bitter uncles, all watching as this idiot who belongs in Western Pennsylvania makes a total *Carrie* of himself.

"I'm so sorry," I say, soft, picking up my bookbag. I pull my new Yankees hat back on so hard, hoping that perhaps some of the magic skills of these brilliant New York kids—these jugglers and flutists—might have rubbed off on stupid Nate Foster. That maybe if I tug this hat on hard enough, down over my entire face, it might make me disappear, or turn me into a rabbit. Ninety bucks Uncle Robert Poppins has a delicious Crock-Pot recipe for stewed rabbit, and a *hundred* bucks he'd cook me and feed the result to Nephew Shawn.

I'm just about to spin on myself and hightail it to the elevators when the casting assistant woman pins my hand to the table, shouting: "Listen up, everyone," shooting me daggers and pulling back her blonde-ringlet hair into a nervous twist. She turns her Starbucks over and spills a remaining gulp all over my lie of an application. "Unless you've got an adult to vouch for you today, don't waste our time. This is *Broadway*," and she leans over, pulling the dripping audition-form out from the garbage, and says (as loudly as anyone has ever said anything, as loudly as the shade of red she used to X out my application), "This isn't *Jankburg, Pennsylvania.*"

"I'll vouch for him," I hear.

The hallway falls even more still, if possible, and from sixteen floors below us a siren whirs past, and you can practically hear the flap of a pigeon's wings from outside the window.

"I can vouch for this boy."

And when I turn, it isn't my imagination talking, or Mrs. Rylance or Uncle Robert.

It's a woman with Mom's nose and Mom's chin and Mom's sad almond eyes, but with better hair, straighter and trendier, and an umbrella and rain boots and the look of a thousand lost dreams all over her shoulders.

"Aunt Heidi."

Explanation Time

We find another corner.

These audition studios are a series of corners, hallways connecting to hallways, like an Escher drawing, a staircase becoming an upside-down door. I have a hunch there might be no actual rooms at all, that when you walk into the "audition studio," it's actually just a direct drop-off to the street below.

And that's what I'm staring at, frozen: an ant path of cabs, a city of yellow where everything would be grey back home.

"Well, long time no see, Nathan," Aunt Heidi says, clicking one of those free pens people get at banks, *click click click.*

"I'm—I can't believe this," I say, turning from the window. I'm not sure what I am most: embarrassed or freaked out or just knocked to my senses by seeing a forgotten blood relative. Someone I haven't laid eyes on since I was a toddler. Someone I only really recognize from the pictures Mom keeps hidden. "I'm really sorry I never thanked you for all the cool cards you sent me," I say.

"Yeah, well," Heidi says, taking off her rain boots and pulling up two wool socks. Wool socks: *that* would've been smart to pack. "Most aunts probably send money, so don't be too hard on yourself, Nathan."

"Nate, now," I want to say, "I just go by Nate, now," but I don't want to stutter, so I just go, "Uh."

Heidi puts her rain boots back on and looks me up and down, just like Libby did in my yard right before sending me off on my maiden moron voyage. But Heidi's eyes are more concerned. Judgmental. "Nathan, what were you *thinking*?"

"You ran away from Pittsburgh yourself, Aunt Heidi," I want to say, "and tried to make it in the big city, so don't look at me like that," but instead I say, "I dunno."

A man comes out of the snack shop, holding a banana and a packet of Protein Graham Crackers, whatever those are. I'm starting to get the sense that you can't get anything in New York without something else coming with it: You can't get directions without getting condescended to, and you can't even get graham crackers without somebody injecting them with protein.

"How—how did you know I was here?" I finally say, the most obvious question to lead with but one that begs an answer I don't want to hear.

"Your friend Libby," Heidi says, taking my shoulder and gently pushing me back, so a few grown-up dancers can pass us, "told your older brother."

"She did *what*?" I say, or shriek, and press away from the wall.

"Keep it down, Nathan."

How could Libby do this to me?

"Your brother got injured at some track event," Heidi says, her eyes doing the Manhattan Dart, "and got home early and found your friend Libby going through his underwear drawer." Libby! "It sounded like quite a thing."

"Oh my God," I say. Holy *Cats*! (*Cats* wasn't technically a flop, but Libby says it was, artistically, so it's on our list of alternate swears.) Holy *Cats*, I can't believe Libby would do that, except I can.

"And Anthony asked her what the *heck* was going on, and she broke down and told him everything. That she'd seen an audition for *E.T.*, online, and couldn't make it because her mom would never let her go to New York. Not with—I don't know, I forget."

"Not with her mom's cancer coming back," I say.

"Yes," Heidi says, sighing and sitting down. I follow suit. "And that all Libby wanted was to audition for the part of Elliott's younger sister. And that her good friend Nathan was so sweet, such a sweetheart, that he offered to go all the way to New York City to drop off her headshot and résumé in a manila envelope, and to bring a CD of the two of you doing some duet."

Not *some* duet. "I'd Give It All for You" from Jason Robert Brown's seminal *Songs for A New World.* We recorded it in the soprano key, even though it's usually for a (normal) guy's and girl's voices. On us, it ended up sounding like a female rock ballad. But still.

I know exactly the CD Libby would've secretly packed for me.

"Apparently you're quite a bold friend, Nathan, but what were you *thinking*?"

"Mom is going to kill me," I say.

"So it is true?"

"Is what true?" I say. A hip-hop dance class begins in a studio directly behind us. That, or a really, really angry guy has started sledgehammering the wall, such is the way the music pulses. If it *is* a guy with a sledgehammer, I hope he finds the spot right where my head is resting.

"Is it true that you came all the way here for your friend? That she actually sent you with a package of her materials?"

I reach into my bookbag and pull out the manila

envelope, sliding it open, and I lift a piece of paper that says, "You're only reading this if there was an emergency and I had to cover for you. Good luck, prince."

I put the paper back in and realize there is no duet, no headshot of Libby, no résumé or CD.

That Libby knows she is six years too old for Elliott's younger sister.

That she has neither the right body for the part nor the right voice. Libby's is a husky, throaty torch voice.

And forget all that, even: between you and me, Libby only acts for *fun*. She's the world's biggest theater *fan*, but she doesn't want to be the world's biggest theater star. Libby wants to be the world's biggest theater star's agent.

Libby wants to be . . . *my* agent.

"Yes, Aunt Heidi," I say. I lie. "Yes, I came all the way here for Libby." I did in a way. I did it for us, and Libby and I are practically one.

"Well, we've got to get you back on the bus, then," Aunt Heidi says. "Come on."

From down six sets of halls, I can hear the mean Starbucks-dumping casting assistant shouting for the next fifty children to line up. And to have gotten all the way here, to have survived the night and two slices of awful pizza, to return to Libby having not even stood in front of the director of the musical: I wouldn't be her hero, and I have to return her hero. Even a fallen one.

"What time is it?" I say to Aunt Heidi.

She looks at her cell phone. "Late enough. *Way* late enough."

"Okay. Okay. Listen: I think there's a one forty-five bus, and I'm already in trouble anyway. Mom's already going to kill me. So maybe I could hang out at the studio just a little longer, and, I dunno . . . while I'm here, peek my head in and sing a song or something, myself. Once I—uh—drop Libby's CD off."

"Nathan," Heidi says, holding her coat tight around the neck, "your mom doesn't even know you're here." She shakes her head. "And she doesn't *have* to. Anthony found my phone number at the back of your mom's address book, since she's the only person in the world who still has a handwritten address book, and he called me. And he told me to get you home."

To save his own butt, I think to myself, but actually: Wow, he could have just called Mom and Dad at the Greenbrier Hotel, interrupting their anniversary vacation to rat me out.

"Is he okay? Did you find out how bad his track accident was?"

"No, something about a strained or sprained calf or

something, but the connection was bad." And then—I don't know why, who can ever tell with grown-ups?—Heidi bursts into tears. "Oh, God, Nathan, I'm sorry. I just—I didn't ask for this." She shouts above the ongoing hip-hop class. "I know I'm the worst aunt and that I disappeared, but your mom never wanted me around. I was never—I shouldn't be saying this to a twelve-year-old."

"Don't worry, Aunt Heidi. I'm nearly fourteen."

She laughs, her throaty cry intermingling in a weird duet with minor hyperventilation. "Oh, Nathan, you look so much like your dad. I can't believe how much you've grown to look like him."

Great. The genes of a janitor.

"Tell me—oh, Nathan, tell me you're not actually here to audition *yourself*. Did you come all the way here to audition for this show, honestly now?"

I take her in. She's beautiful, actually. Maybe a little soft on the sides, but her almond eyes are matched by a lovely old-fashioned face, shaped like a guitar pick, all curves leading dramatically to a small chin with a big mouth. The only one in the family that's just like minc. Her big expressive mouth, now spilling with something that sounds like a confession. We were raised partially Catholic, so I'd know.

"Aunt Heidi, I—my whole life, all I've wanted was to come here." Technically just the last three years, but who cares about anything other than Count Chocula when you're under ten? "To experience it just once. And I need to get back down the hall and get in line, and have that chance. I just—I will regret it forever if I don't."

"Nathan, I'm sorry—I really am. But I need to get you back on that bus before things get . . . even messier."

The hip-hop music cuts off abruptly, followed by quiet applause, and I say too loudly, "If Mom has already disowned you, what's the worst thing that could happen here?"

Whoops.

"I need—I need to . . ." But Heidi edits herself, running into a girls' bathroom just beyond.

Superwhoops.

Legs Diamond! in fact. (1988, ran for sixty-four performances, which sounds like forever to me but is considered a flop, here. Starred an Australian with a legendary lisp. Flop. Big-ol' flop.)

And here's my chance. Here's my chance to escape into the rabbit warren of hallways, back to the lineup of kids, to secure my place as number ninety-one, now publicly endorsed by an adult (even if she's in the bathroom crying).

I'll probably get looked up and down and laughed at by "the team" and released right after the type-out, unfit to audition for *E.T.* And then at least I can go back to Jankburg with the confirmation that I shouldn't even be dreaming this dream, and just weave myself firmly back into the tapestry of local boredom. Of the greys of Jankburg.

And when I stand to fill up my water bottle and pop a lozenge and check that my audition music hasn't wrinkled, I break into tears too. The weight of it all—the realization that Anthony covered for me and Libby covered for me; that Aunt Heidi has to see her stupid nephew who looks like her stupid janitor brother-in-law; that she probably avoided me for years for this very reason, probably because I remind her too much of all the people in my family who are too closed-minded to accept that she had a New York dream too; that she wouldn't work at Flora's Floras and wanted, instead, something more for herself, something different and less grey? Well, it all makes me cry.

I pass a strange wicker hallway mirror and see my face. My oily face that is indeed starting to trade freckles for zits.

And you know what? Aunt Heidi was wrong. I don't look like my dad. I look like her.

"Nate." She appears, getting my name right, getting me, and I turn around to her. She is looking at me like I'm poisoned, like I'm the famous cream dress she stole out of Mom's closet, for Homecoming, and which ended up stained with red wine by the end of the night. Legendary family story. And Heidi had to bring it back to my mom, sobbing, apologizing.

And that's how she's looking at me. Like I'm that dress, stained and irretrievable.

"Aunt Heidi, I'm so sorry," I say. She reaches to touch my arm. And you know how when you've just pulled it together but then somebody gives you the slightest touch, not even a hug, but shows you the littlest kindness? And you just lose it again? "Don't," I say, "please, don't. Please."

"Come on," she says, looking at her watch, "we need to get you on the next bus. Like, *now*." I pick up my bookbag and slot Libby's emergency manila envelope back in.

"Are those . . . lozenges?" Aunt Heidi says.

"What?" I say, wiping my horrible zitty nose against my horrible plaid shirt, the shirt of a pirate out to prove that he doesn't care what people think of him. Except I do. I do terribly.

"Did you pack lozenges for your trip?"

"Yes." (And I even thought of it before Libby did.)

"Because that's what Broadway people—what—*carry* on them?" Heidi says, smiling or something.

"I dunno, yes. Yes?"

"And you've got your water bottle, and"—she pulls back the zipper of my bookbag—"twenty-four Entenmann's Donuts?"

"Twenty." I'd had four on the bus ride. "Actually, sixteen." I had several today, and one at the rest stop after I thought the guy was going to kill me in the bathroom; when he was only handing me Libby's brilliant escape note.

"That sounds about right," Heidi says. "Most of my actor friends eat donuts all day and drink water." She clears her throat and brushes the hair off her shoulders. "When they're not doing yoga," I think she says, quietly.

"I guess we ought to really scram, huh," I say, composing my voice, "if I want to swing by Applebee's before the bus?"

Even though I'll hate myself if I don't audition. Even though Libby fell on her sword for me, and I didn't even earn it.

Heidi doesn't say anything, pausing like my head might be on fire. "Come on," she finally says, "let's get out of here," and she leads me to the bank of elevators.

And when the elevator dings, another round of children get out; one relevant boy in particular holds a stack of music and a beautiful, professional color headshot, topped only by his audition song: "Bigger Isn't Better." Same as mine but probably sung like a real boy, with friends. Just as all of this happens, the blonde casting assistant woman yells out, "Anthony Foster? Number ninety-one, are you here or not?"

Her voice is ragged, the ripped chords of an Eat'n Park hostess back home. Of somebody who has been calling my number for the last ten minutes, I can hear, and is as ready to give up on me as I am.

I look at Aunt Heidi.

"Anthony?" she says.

"I"—I fight back tears, my face a leaking boat in a storm—"I lied. And I used Anthony's fake ID."

The boy with my song and the nice headshot passes us and snickers, and finally there's something here that I can relate to: being laughed at. I would give anything to be like him. He's probably a whole three years younger than me. Back when nobody at school had gotten the growth spurt that could give them the strength and confidence to steal your lunch, to bury it in the playground sand, to not even eat your turkey sandwich with too much mayonnaise that you had to wake up and make for yourself that morning.

"Just a second," Heidi calls down the hall, leaving my side, pushing past the snickering boy. "Just a second, please." The hallway stops squirming and looks at her. "Anthony Foster is here. Anthony Foster is going to audition."

I swallow and blink, and pop a lozenge, uncapping my water bottle and spilling half the contents down my shirt in a hasty chug. Heidi walks up to the casting assistant and exchanges some words, her head shaking a lot and hands planted firmly on her hips. She races back to me.

"Come on," she says, pushing the down elevator button. "We've got twenty minutes until your group goes in."

"Where—what are we doing?" and Heidi doesn't even allow the next elevator car of people to debark. She just burrows through, like the hedgehog Dad hates in our backyard.

"We're getting you a new outfit," Heidi says, hitting the lobby button and pulling me into the elevator car, the locals staring. "No nephew of mine is auditioning for *E.T.: The Musical* in that outfit."

And we're off.

Buying Clothes with an Aunt I Barely Know

"What do kids wear these days? Would you be insulted if I took you to Old Navy?"

We're dashing, cutting through pedestrians and into the street, not only *not* obeying basic traffic laws but also basic human decency protocol; twice, I watch Aunt Heidi flip off cab drivers who almost take her out.

"No, Old Navy is fine, I guess. I dunno. Mom buys all my clothes." I probably shouldn't mention Mom too often, since it's clear Aunt Heidi thinks Mom can't stand her.

"Your mom can't stand me," Aunt Heidi says, hitting another sidewalk edge and doing a New Yorker's version of looking both ways (not looking both ways). She takes a quick moment to check on me, behind her, the brim of my Yankees cap whipping wind into my eyes. I've never run fast enough to get wind in my eyes.

"You're quite a sprinter, Aunt Heidi, and I'm sure Mom *can* stand you. Just because she doesn't mention you ever doesn't mean anything."

Then, cutting through an alley and coming out alongside a shop that *only* sells caramel popcorn (seriously, you've got to see it to believe it; I bet they have entire stores here that only sell bubble gum or Twizzlers, too; a great town), Madison Square Garden towers before us.

"Holy moley," I say, and Aunt Heidi laughs and says, "Aw, Nate, is a stadium making you homesick for Pittsburgh?"

In Pittsburgh, you can barely cross the street without passing a stadium or a football fan or a tailgate party. Everyone is always celebrating victory or arguing about defeat.

"I was actually more impressed," I say to Heidi, my eyes trained on the massive Madison Square Garden lights and the ads for cell phones and trips to Bermuda, "because Libby has a Playbill from a production of *A Christmas Carol* that played here."

"Okay," Heidi says, finally stopping to catch her breath. I follow the lead and practically fall over, like a machine set to crazy spin mode that's all of a sudden been switched off with no cooldown. "Old Navy is across the street," she says, not even panting. "We've got to be back to the audition in, like, seventeen minutes."

We've done all of *this* in three minutes? Three minutes for stadium sightings and almost getting killed by cabs, and flipping them off, and seeing a grown man in a leotard with a trained rat on his head (that happened two blocks ago, but it whirred by so fast I barely had time to include it in the text)?

"Nate!" Heidi says. "Goodness, you're a daydreamer. Snap out of it." And she takes me by the hand and walks me across the street, in an orderly, weirdly law-abiding way. "I used to date the cop on the corner," she says, "and I don't want to attract attention by jaywalking."

We get to the boys' section and it overwhelms me. I hate clothes shopping and, even more, having to make any decision.

"What size are you?" she says.

"Eek. Whatever Mom buys. Probably boys'."

"Boys' *what*?"

"Just that? Just . . . boys' size?"

"Oy, Nate," she says, pulling back the collar on my plaid Montego's shirt to inspect the tag. "Who dressed you in this, for goodness' sake?"

"Oh, this was an emergency purchase." I open my bookbag and untwist the plastic bag, with my hometown clothes now bunched into a wet fist, then pull out my navy polo. "But this is what I usually wear."

"I don't even want to know," Aunt Heidi says,

inspecting the dripping sleeves. "Okay, we need to find you a boys' medium. This says 'husky' but no nephew of mine is wearing a husky." I like that she's taking ownership of me.

"Keep in mind," I say, "that the role I'm auditioning for is Elliott, the wise-beyond-his-years sensitive son of a single mother. He is enchanted by aliens. And bums around the house in sweats a lot, according to the film. So maybe nothing too fancy?"

Heidi holds up a black-and-pink striped shirt from a sale rack. "I have no idea how to dress a child. What do children wear?"

"Aunt Heidi, when was the last time you hung out with a thirteen-year-old?" I say.

She rolls her eyes. "We have to get you back uptown, but let's just say my last adolescent experience didn't go well. I was down to the end to play the mother in a canker-sore commercial—it was the only time I've ever been too *young* for anything, believe me—and lost out to a woman who ended up getting a recurring on one of those sappy hospital dramas."

So she *is* an actress! Mom never told me but I knew; I just *knew* that nobody would leave Jankburg, and the easy security of a job at the family flower shop, to move to New York and work in the floral industry. Nothing seems to grow here, nothing outdoors anyway. The only time I've seen anything green, it was the palm tree in the pot at the audition.

"Have you been in other TV commercials?"

"A few, a million years ago," Heidi says, holding a red T-shirt up to me. "But I gave that all up for the glories of a waitress gig. Let's not talk about it." And then I'm being led to a dressing room. I can't believe she's been in commercials! "Okay, Nate, put this T-shirt on, and take off that hat—like, forever, honestly—and I'm going to find you a pair of jeans." She crouches down in front of me. "Are you allowed to be left alone in a dressing room without me? You don't like, need me to button your pants or anything, do you?"

"Aunt Heidi, I'm *thirteen*, not three."

Mom has, of course, never left me alone in a dressing room, and certainly not one in the middle of Manhattan (where musicals are so big, they have to play at sports arenas), but Aunt Heidi needn't know all this. She's distraught already, it's clear, over the canker-sore commercial flashback.

And here I am, staring into a dressing-room mirror, my hat off and the brim—much tighter than I'd realized—having branded a red rim across my forehead, giving me the overall look of a post-lobotomy gradeschooler who, as a final wish before the infection sets in, gets to visit the World's Biggest Old Navy, just once.

"Nate," Heidi says, knocking on the door. "Are you all finished in there?"

All finished? I just got here. My God, everything is warp speed in New York.

"Just a sec, Aunt Heidi," I say, and whip the plaid tent off over my head and avoid looking too close at my soft body in the hard light. Heidi flips a pair of jeans—miraculously, just my size—over the top of the door, and I emerge for her to inspect me.

She claps and giggles, playing absent-mindedly with her hair. "Oh my God, you look adorable. Take back what I said about you looking like your dad—you look like a doll. Oh, God, I see the appeal of dressing a child."

I spin on myself and wonder if it's a good thing to look like a doll. "Are you sure these clothes aren't too tight, Aunt Heidi?"

"No, they actually *fit.* I'm sure you all dress in sizes that are way too big, back home. This actually looks human on you." She's pulling me to a cash register. "What's up with your forehead?"

The lobotomy.

"Oh, my hat, the Yankees hat. It was too tight."

Aunt Heidi pays for the whole outfit! "Consider these new clothes a gift," she says, "to make up for all the birthdays I've missed."

"You sent cards," I say, but she's already three paces ahead of me, running again, like we're in a relay and a billion-dollar iTunes gift card is at the finish line.

"Come on!" she shouts, and pulls me into a cab,

announcing "Eighth Avenue at Thirty-sixth." Which I love, which sounds like a real spy-thing to say. I would've gotten in and said, "Take me to the place where children's dreams come true if they aren't eliminated for being too pear shaped or not being able to juggle."

And then, in opposite fashion to our racing-by-foot venture, the cab is suddenly the slowest vehicle I've ever been in, like we're just sitting on an inner tube in traffic and hoping the tide picks up.

"Come on, man," Aunt Heidi says to the driver. She looks over at me. "Are you having, like, any fun?"

Any!?

"Oh, gosh, Aunt Heidi, this is probably the most exciting day of my life." I see a woman purchase a street pretzel and my belly groans, on cue, issuing its vote.

"Are you starving?" Aunt Heidi says, looking at me like I might shatter if she doesn't water me often enough.

"I wouldn't say starving, but I caught sight of a very beautiful Applebee's, back near the Port Authority, and I might want to pop in there for a few fajitas, after."

"Okay," Heidi says, now looking back out the window, again clicking that free bank pen open-shut, *click click click*. "If you're in New York, you are never, *ever* allowed to go to an Applebee's. Like, it's totally off limits."

"Why?" It's one of the great restaurants of our time, I thought.

"Because—just—the only reason to even be here," she says, "the only reason to deal with all the hassle—*come on, man, can you get us there any slower?*—is to also exploit the good stuff. And the good stuff is the local restaurants and the culture and junk."

We come to a red light, and Heidi opens the door and grabs my arm, and just as she's reaching for her purse, I say, "I'll do this, Aunt Heidi," and give the guy a five-dollar bill. It's thrilling.

"Don't ask for any change," Heidi says, thinking I'm not old enough to understand tipping systems. Thinking I've never worked a shift or two at Flora's Floras, and had to get there by taking the bus, and slept through the bus so I had to call a car service. All of that. I'm much more grown up, I think, than Aunt Heidi realizes.

We're back in the elevator, chugging its way up to the sixteenth floor, to the audition. Heidi looks at her cell phone and musses my hair, flicking it this way and that. "You should trim your bangs when you get home. Just an idea."

The doors part and we make a hard right and they're all lined up, all forty-nine of my group. The casting assistant with blonde ringlet hair and a hoarse voice gets up from the desk and walks over to us. "Where the heck is Anthony Foster?"

I raise my hand. "I'm here."

Casting assistant girl goes, "Whoa, costume

change," smiling, amazingly, and then scrunches her face and says, "What's up with your forehead?"

Aunt Heidi takes my bookbag and says, "He just had a final callback for a commercial, and had to wear a really tight hat." She gives my leg a kick, and casting assistant girl says "whatever" and shows me to my place in line, two people ahead of the pretty girl with the flute.

"Okay, listen up," casting assistant girl screams. "You'll all be going in, in one minute. I'm going to need everyone to leave their bags with their guardians or parents, and please hear me on this: If you have a special skill you'd like to show off—I see a few boys have brought skateboards and a girl has a flute—you can bring those items in and set them in the corner of the room."

I look around and wonder if I can show them Libby's emergency note. My special skill is being protected by other children who are smarter than I am.

"Do you have any hidden talents?" Heidi asks.

"Nah," I say. "Not really. I mean, I *can* hold my breath for three minutes underwater." It's my one expertise that even *orbits* the world of sports; Anthony tried to drown me once.

"Okay," Heidi says, "you don't have to mention that if they ask."

"Please," casting assistant girl says, "stay exactly in

this lineup when you walk in the door, children. Like going to the potty with your entire class. Because the creatives have already had a long morning, and we don't want any of you beautiful children to get lost in the shuffle."

"This girl," Aunt Heidi whispers to me, but not quite quietly enough, frankly, "is the reason I stopped acting."

And the door swings open.

The long flowy man comes out, his face flush and his blouse wrinkled into a fret, and he looks as if he's already given up on the entire project. That some time in the last hour he became so annoyed at something—maybe the juggling brothers threw a ball at his head—that "the creatives," whatever that means, had a meeting and decided *E.T.: The Musical* was a horrible idea all along. That *Close Encounters* would have made for more compelling material. An entire song about mashed potato spaceships.

"Lock and load, kiddos!" the long flowy man yells instead, turning his face into a mask of comedy (in an overly rehearsed way). I follow the boy in front of me and turn back to Aunt Heidi, and she gives me the thumbs-up, and we're in.

God, I have to pee.

It's Not Like in the Movies

The room is horrible—let me say that now.

Sure, exciting. Blah blah blah, the mystique and intrigue of an interview. Yadda yadda, the pulsing energy that keeps you aloft even as you're crashing from an overnight bus trip and an Old Navy hike.

The room is horrible.

Wild, blinking overhead lights, and the reek of a root cellar (in a bad way), and floor-to-ceiling mirrors that force you to stare yourself down. To see that underbite. To measure yourself up against every other kid standing here. Every other flute player.

"Okay, children," the long flowy man says, clapping at us. There's a lot of clapping here, that's for sure, and not the audience kind; the shut-up kind. "Drop your stuff over by Sammy the pianist."

Sammy the pianist looks up from his iPhone and smiles a crooked, tired smile.

"And then I need you all to line up, from numbers fifty-one through one hundred like Beckany instructed outside." Casting assistant girl has a name: Beckany. The sort of thing my dad would call "a fool's name." This gives me a nice bonding moment with Dad, which happens about once every thirteen years.

I'm the only kid, it seems, who *doesn't* have some instrument or special pair of shoes to drop off by Sammy, and I'm standing in the middle of the room taking in the adults, more of them than I thought would be here. They are clearly led by an important bald man, pacing, with a set of eyeglasses perched on his tree-branch nose, and another set on his scalp, and a *third* set, sunglasses, swinging around his neck on a flamboyant chain of blood-red crystals.

The bald man is being followed by a very skinny woman (a "She needs a burger" kind of woman, my mom would say) with spiked auburn hair. And though she's not traditionally pretty, she's obviously been in show business long enough to know how to dress herself up, donning more makeup than most groups of friends would spread among themselves to put together a haunted house to scare the little kids on the block.

Maybe I'll go as *this* woman for Halloween.

At the front of the room, as the other children mill about, I see two young men, somewhere between older-than-Anthony and thirty, both of them with tiny beards and clipboards and sweater vests and tight jeans. They're giggling a lot already, commenting back and forth.

And then there's the flowy man, who's rounding up the troops. He looks at me and says, "Okay, everyone, do like number ninety-one is doing and stand in line." He strides up to me with giant, urban strides and grabs my shoulders and pushes me back three feet. "Do just like number ninety-one but stand on the line we have, right here." And he puts me on it: a black stretch of tape, crossing the room. "And let's do this quickly. Your first task is to line up quickly."

This sounds idiotic, of course—who *can't* stand in a line—but you really can't believe how hard it is for these kids. Maybe my special skill is "being in lines first," because the ruckus that ensues, the forty-nine other children trying to find the number of the kid next to him or her? You'd think they were offering ten free cookies and the first of us to line up gets them, such is the screaming and panic.

The redheaded woman with extravagant Rockette legs whistles, like she's herding us, and starts matching kids next to kids.

The long flowy man says, "Yes, let's let Monica do this. This is what dance people do," and the bearded boys laugh really, really hard, like it's the first good joke on a bad Kids' Choice Awards telecast, and in just a moment we are lined up.

Monica really was quite good at herding us.

"So let's do quiet faces," the long flowy man says. "Let's do beautiful quiet faces with little closed mouths."

Everyone shuts up, and Sammy the piano player plays a "ta-da" on the keyboard. We kids aren't sure if we're allowed to laugh, but the bearded assistant boys howl (*really* scream) at Sammy's "ta-da," and the screaming of the bearded boys makes us kids titter.

"My name," the long flowy man says, "is Rex Rollins. And I am the casting director of *E.T.: The Musical.*"

The boy next to me applauds, and that makes a few other kids clap. I can see it all in the giant, wall-size mirrors stretched in front of us (*what* did Aunt Heidi do to my bangs?). Rex Rollins the casting director does a curtsy, something wildly girly, and that makes the bearded boys hoot so hard that I think one of their beards is going to pop off, like, literally.

"We'll be here all day," Monica the dance person says, winking at Rex Rollins.

"Let me introduce the team today," Rex says. "You already met Sammy at the piano," and a wise-guy kid yells out "ta-da." Dear Lord.

I'm getting the idea that "the team" is just a

bunch of adults who look like caricature versions of normal people; the Pittsburgh version of Rex Rollins would be a dad in not such a loud floral print, and the Pittsburgh version of Monica would be a math teacher who would never wear those high heels; and I don't think we have a Pittsburgh version of the bearded boys, who are standing awfully close to one another and clearly writing things on their clipboards to make each other laugh, like we can't tell. Like we're idiots. "The team" just stands there beaming like they've all won the Nobel Peace Prize for Musical Theater.

"And you've met Monica," Rex Rollins says, "who is assisting the very talented, very dashing Olivier Award–winning Mr. Garret Charles. Our choreographer."

This, strangely, *doesn't* get applause, perhaps because big bald Mr. Garret Charles looks as if he eats children for lunch.

"And Mark with a *k* and Marc with a *c* are our helpers"—Mark and Marc, the bearded boys, flash smiles that could outwatt the moon on a clear night—"and that's it for today. Our assistant director is running a little late."

Assistant director? I'm not even meeting the *director* director? What is this I'm auditioning for, a dance concert?

"So," Rex says, "please stand with your feet together"—

"Parallel first position," Monica shouts, tapping nails against her clipboard. She brings her toes and heels together in a single dramatic click, overemphasizing a military way of standing straight. "Parallel *first*."

"*Dance* terms," Rex says, smiling a huge smile from a mouth that isn't as bright as Mark's or Marc's but looks, instead, like it enjoys seven or eight hoagies per weekend. "Stand in *parallel first* and make sure we can see your numbered name tag, and stand *very still* and we'll be quick about this."

"Can I just say something?" Mr. Garret Charles says, stepping forward. The room goes edgy, nervous, and a light flickers off. He has a British accent so over the top you'd think he was making fun of *Harry Potter*. "These situations can be very stressful, very difficult. We are looking for something so specific for *E.T.: The Musical*. It is a movie that is beloved across seas, and oceans." His assistant, Monica, is nodding gigantically like she's rewarding a particularly feeble dog. "And the task of casting such a work calls for a specific image in an audience's mind."

"Aliens!" a stupid boy shouts.

"That's right, young man," Garret Charles says, and then squints at the boy's number, pinned to his stupid hip, and whispers something to Monica. Who very clearly draws a line through the boy's name on her clipboard.

"Aliens, yes," Garret Charles continues, his accent growing thicker by the syllable, and bordering on German. "But also of a certain era and locale: of the eighties, in a dusty California town that isn't accustomed to outside visitors. And our task is to honor the work of Steven Spielberg, of his glorious little film that is *really* about—does anyone perceive what it's really about?"

I expect the stupid boy to shout "Aliens!" again, but instead a girl wearing pink ballet tights raises her hand. Garret Charles points to her, and she says, "It's about a boy and his friend."

Rex Rollins, eating a Dorito by the piano, looks around and shakes his head, really digging this girl's answer, and calls to Garret Charles, "I love the simplicity of that."

"Yes," Garret Charles says, "it's about friendship—and about how fast that friend can leave you. Indeed, young lady. So please, look from child to child, next to you, greet them as if at mass, and introduce yourself quickly. Because we'll be cutting this group down by at least half, and I want you to make a friend and then learn, and see, how quickly all that can change."

We stand there, dumbfounded, but Rex Rollins claps at us and we switch back on.

I turn to the girl next to me, who has a set of braces so sprawling you could probably tie them to

Dad's fishing rod and hook a shark, and say, "Hi, I'm Nate," and she says, "I'm Cindy, this is so wild." And then I turn to the little boy next to me and say, "Hi, I'm Nate," and he says, "I pee-peed my pants a little."

And I'm about to.

Rex Rollins claps at us again, to quiet the rumble, and Monica and Garret begin at one end of the room, near the smaller numbers. They walk the line, slowly, eyeing each of us like a pair of drill sergeants. Occasionally they confer, but mostly Monica makes one of two marks on her clipboard—either a checkmark, I think, or just a line, a little dash.

The room is a cluster of fidget, every three or four children practically breaking out of his or her own skin, hopping. But not me.

I am standing stone still, riveted to this day. The rain begins again, tapping against the window like an intruder or a warning, and finally, at the very peak of the room's growing hum, a child begins hiccupping. Garret Charles turns very pink and bites his lower lip. His nostrils flare, and he switches the pair of glasses on his forehead for the pair on his nose, and he walks out the door behind me. And slams it.

Monica takes a deep breath and says, "I need *everyone*"—her head whipping to the hiccupping child, the same stupid boy, I see, who yelled "Aliens!" earlier—"to be completely still. Whether or not you realize it—and

I think this is a lesson that's worth learning as a child—every moment in life is an audition. Every moment, and not just when you're dancing or singing for us, if you get that far, is a moment to show who you are. And what I see here are a bunch of children who are wearing good little outfits and good little shoes but can't stand still." God, does she love to talk. "And that's the first thing Garret Charles asked—was for you to please stand still."

He actually didn't say that. Garret Charles actually gave us a generic monologue about the dust of California in the eighties. It was Rex *Rollins* the large casting director who asked us kids to stand still, almost twenty minutes ago, and *he's* the most hyperactive person in here: swilling away at his third can of Diet Coke and pawing a string cheese into his mouth like he's a bear who found his first salmon after a drought. But whatever.

Garret Charles comes back, and when I turn to see him enter, I catch sight of the clock. I'm going to be toast if I don't make it out of here in the next hour. Mom and Dad still don't know I'm in New York, and Libby can only cover for me so long.

God, I hope his calf is okay. If he's medically hobbled by this mysterious track injury, he's going to be home a lot more, and that means our shared bathroom is going to be a real negotiation that I will lose every time.

"You," Monica says to me, suddenly standing right in front of me. "Daydreamer. Where are you from?"

"Oh, uh—" Do I look like that much of a foreigner? Can they smell the grey on me, the fumes of Jankburg? "I'm from Pennsylvania."

"How old are you?" Garret Charles says, his eyes beady. God, have they *all* seen my coffee-stained application? Do they know I lied about being twenty-one?

"I'm as old as you need the character of Elliott to be," I'm about to say, to steal that boy's line from the elevator, but instead I go, "I'm thirteen. I'm thirteen, sir."

Monica laughs at my saying "sir," muttering something like, "I bet this kid thinks you're a knight, Garret."

And she makes no mark at all by my name, moving on to Cindy with the braces. Cindy does a strange bow to them, and that's all it takes for Monica to scratch right through her name on the clipboard.

"Do you think they just *eliminated* me," Cindy says just as soon as Garret Charles and Monica are on to the next victim, and I say, "Nah, I think they probably really fell for that formal bow you gave them," and she flashes her big scary braces at me again, and I actually let out a yelp, sounding like Mom's horrible dog, Tippy.

The only other real notable, in the walk-down

Garret Charles is doing, is a child at the far end of the room who begins to cry when they get to him. He, too, appears to have pee-peed his pants, just like the poor boy to my left. Either that or he popped a water balloon in his shorts. (Unlikely.) The boy is excused—one of the bearded boys taking him by the hand, out to the waiting area—and then Rex Rollins puts his Diet Coke down on Sammy's piano and begins to clap again, to quiet a room down that has already become so quiet, the clapping itself makes another little girl begin to cry; suddenly everyone seems to be crying.

"There are many different types of children for many different types of shows," Rex Rollins begins, and I can see that he's given this speech about a billion times. "So if your number is not one of the numbers we call in just a moment—if you aren't asked to stay for longer, today—I want you to keep in mind that there are lots of opportunities for all sorts of children."

Really? What kind of shows need girls with horrible braces, or little boys who pee their pants? Or me?

Garret Charles crouches low against the mirror, with Monica, and flips through the pages on her clipboard fervently. He's actually squatting so deeply that I can't help but stare; this dramatic Yoga pose is the first evidence that he must have really been a good dancer once. Garret Charles is, like, at least ten years older than Dad, and if Dad tried that kind of crouch, his knees would probably fly right off his legs, across the dining room.

Monica reaches into her purse and pulls out a cell phone, hightailing it to the door. Doesn't she want to watch our faces as we're kept or cut? Isn't the chief interest of being in charge that you can enjoy the crushed or giddy reactions of your subjects? I won't ever understand adults, I swear.

"Number fifty-nine, do you have any special skills?" Mark, one of the bearded casting assistants, says. Garret Charles has called Mark over, in Monica's absence, and is now whispering into his ear.

"I'm a straight-A student," number fifty-nine says, a boy whose socks are pulled so high, he may've actually lost a bet with someone.

Mark laughs and scratches his little beard, saying, "That's wonderful, but I think Mr. Charles is looking for special skills that could apply to a Broadway musical."

"This *is* Broadway after all, children," Garret Charles says, tilting his head down to peer through the tiny glass of his tiny glasses, perched on his tiny sharp nose that could probably pick a lock if tilted the right way.

God, his accent is something else. If I tried to impersonate a British person, like that, Libby would tell me I'm working too hard and ruining the scene.

"Let the words do the work," she said to me once during a two-week summer intensive on *Arden of Faversham.*

"Well," number fifty-nine continues, "I'm a straight-A student *and* I played Seymour in my middle school's production of *Little Shop of Horrors, Jr.* And my parents said I was the best thing in it, and so did my history teacher, Mrs. Cahoon, and that was the last thing she ever saw, because she was killed in a hot-air balloon accident in France."

"Oh, my," Mark says, and moves on to the next number on his list. I've figured it out already: They're only following up with the children who they haven't made their final decision about. Whose fate is hovering in the air like a bee.

"Number eighty-eight, do you have any special skills?" And really, just like that, number eighty-eight performs a forward handspring, landing in the splits. The room erupts into applause, but number eighty-eight isn't done, not by the half of it, calling to Sammy at the piano, "Do you know 'Slow Boat to China'?"

And Sammy, quite amazingly, *does* seem to (not that I know that song), and begins thumping out a beat. And number eighty-eight—still in the splits!—spins out of them, onto her back, and yells "Faster!" to Sammy, which gets a nice big laugh out of Mark and Marc, the bearded boys. Number eighty-eight ends up—and I'd need to watch the whole thing on slow-mo to really understand how she even *thought* of it, let alone pulled it off—balanced on her chin, legs in the air, arms out in an upside-down T.

Number eighty-eight flips up to her feet, which had shone in the air, shone as she spun, glittering in the light. I hear the clickety-clack of metal, and—my God—number eighty-eight is in tap shoes, launching into a series of time steps so accomplished, I feel at this point like I should be paying money to watch the routine.

And just as soon as she's done, somehow back-hand-springing directly into line, her feet in a perfect "parallel first" position, Garret Charles makes a small notation next to her name on the clipboard.

And in order, I suppose, to destroy her, he simply says, "Okay."

If an act like *hers* only gets an "okay," what the heck am *I* going to get when they get to *my* name? A death threat?

By now, with Monica back inside the room, Mark scurries out of the way and Garret stands. His body snaps and crackles in so many places, he sounds like a bowl of Rice Krispies. My stomach growls.

"Number ninety-one," Monica calls out to me. "Any special skills?"

I clear my throat and catch a quick look at myself

in the mirror: that new red shirt and those jeans, my boring new slip-on shoes. Everything feels like it's a size too small for me.

"I can walk on my knees."

And I really can.

When Libby and I workshopped our two-person *Fiddler on the Roof*, for the private performance we put on for her mom right when she started getting sick, I decided to stage the famous Bottle Dance. In the musical *Fiddler on the Roof*, a rambunctious Jewish father has to marry off his daughters, and during one of the ceremonies, the town villagers place a series of real live glass bottles atop their heads, pushed into the divots of their felt hats. Arm in arm, these men—because what woman would be willing to look this ridiculous?—perform a series of leg dips and crawls—knee walks—all the while making sure their bottles stay securely balanced on top of their head.

"I can walk on my knees, or crawl on them, I mean," I hear myself say.

Garret Charles hands the clipboard to Monica and says, "Well, this shall be interesting."

"Sammy," I want to call out, "Keep playing 'Slow Boat to China,' but reroute that canoe to Russia," but instead I just step forward, out of line. Cindy with the braces snorts. I start to bend my knees when, with a pinch, the new jeans stop me, tugging at the crotch.

Too tight to perform any kind of trick.

My big chance, ruined by denim.

"Children: a lesson," Monica says. "When auditioning for a new musical, it's very, very important to wear clothing that allows for movement."

"I could—I could change," I offer. "I could put on a pair of shorts," thinking I might pop my head into the hall to scream at Aunt Heidi, "GET BACK TO OLD NAVY AND JAYWALK IN FRONT OF YOUR EX-BOYFRIEND THE COP IF YOU HAVE TO, JUST GET ME A PAIR OF LOOSELY FITTING SHORTS THAT ALLOW UNINHIBITED, JEWISH-WEDDING-DANCE-TYPE MOVEMENT."

Garret Charles looks at me, peering again through his glasses, and says, "Changing your garments won't be necessary."

Mine is the last number they call today, the team so clearly distraught at the lack of special skills displayed before them, they're just going to chuck our whole group.

"Okay, children!" Rex Rollins says, taking the clipboard from Monica. "Please take your belongings into the hallway, and wait with your parents for just a moment. We'll confer and then come out to announce the next step. But you all did a sensational job!"

Ridiculous. Only *one* of us did anything near a sensational job—spinning on her chin—and the rest of us either peed our pants or couldn't move in them.

When I return to Heidi (after finally running to the bathroom myself), she looks up from her cell phone and rises from a creaking wicker seat. "What's wrong, Nate?" I suppose I look like I'm about to cry.

I suppose I'm about to cry.

I suppose I cry.

I'm crying.

"It was horrible. They hated me," I say. "It wasn't anything like what I thought an audition would be. They were just—just *looking* at us, and trying to intimidate us."

Heidi just stands there, probably afraid to touch me in case it makes me cry harder.

Rex Rollins spills out of the door frame, with Mark and Marc flanking him like slices of wheat bread, and—yup—claps his hands at us.

"First off, congratulations to the parents for raising a bunch of wonderful kiddos!" One of the moms shouts "Hear, hear!" and earns polite applause. "As I already said in the room, casting a new musical is such a delicate process because there are so few slots for so many kids. We could probably cast the national tour of *E.T.* just out of this group of fifty kiddos alone!"

A dad looks up from his BlackBerry and says, "When does the national tour go out?" And Rex Rollins says, "It was just an expression! We've got to get this show open on Broadway first!"

The "Hear, hear!" mom yells, "I smell a Tony Award!" And the whole hallway is just so confusing to me, everyone pretending to be friends when really nobody is friends, when nobody wants anything but this chance, this job.

"Will the following numbers please stay," Rex Rollins says. "You'll be asked to sing in our afternoon group, at two p.m., after the creative team takes their lunch." And I swear, one of the pee-pee-pants boys yells out, "You deserve a wonderful lunch!" and Rex Rollins does his signature curtsy.

The BlackBerry dad isn't so into this guy, and holds his daughter tight.

"Breathe, Nate," Heidi says, and hands me back my bookbag. And that's when I see it, hanging from a wire ring looped into a zipper: my lucky rabbit foot from Libby. I squat and, despite hands that are sweaty and shaking, unspool the ring from the zipper. I hold the rabbit foot so tight that I bet some distant, footless bunny must be wincing or shouting.

I remember the day Libby gave it to me: we'd arrived at sixth-grade drama class to find it had been replaced by a study hall. That another arts program was axed, deemed "frivolous" by the school board. We were supposed to be doing *Peter Pan* for the winter musical, and I was basically dying to play the title role, but *it* was canceled too. And when I got home from school that day, crying into my pillow, Libby's shoe careened into my window (our secret hello). She was in the yard below, holding this old rabbit foot. Given to me toward some future fortune.

". . . number ninety, number ninety-three, number ninety-nine, and number one hundred. Please stay."

"Wait," I say, turning to Aunt Heidi, "did they say ninety-one? Did they keep number ninety-one?"

Her face falls, and she just shakes her head. "No, Natey, they didn't. I'm so sorry."

But I can barely make out her words on account of the jubilation around me, children jumping up and down, into and out of their adoring parents' arms. One girl—the tumbler, number eighty-eight from before—actually crawls *up* her father like he's a tree, and ends up atop his shoulders, cock-a-doodle-dooing from on high, to celebrate being kept for the next round of auditions.

This girl would make a heck of a Peter Pan.

"Keep in mind," Rex Rollins says, clapping us quiet, "this is only the first round. And all of the children who were cut today will be totally right for another show."

"Nate," Aunt Heidi says, "I think we ought to get going. Honestly. We've *got* to get you on the next bus to Pittsburgh."

And when we turn the corner into the elevator bank, there's Jordan Rylance, coming back to the studio with his mom in her awful faux-leopard coat. Her mouth lifts and she says, way too loud, "Did you get a callback to sing later, too?" and I just shake my head no, that they didn't see anything worth liking about me.

"Sorry," Jordan says, shoveling a Subway sandwich down his throat.

"Are you," Mrs. Rylance says to my aunt, "Nathan's mom?"

And Heidi, who is holding the elevator door open, says, "No, gosh no," and then looks at me. "I just mean I'd be a terrible mother."

The door starts to close on her, and she motions for me to board the elevator. So much for my lucky rabbit foot. So much for it watching over me and bringing a future fortune.

Through the shutting steel doors, Mrs. Rylance pops in her beaming face and looks right at me: "Well, better luck back in Jankburg, Nathan."

"It's N-n-nate."

"I have to get him to the bus!" Heidi says, about to swat Mrs. Rylance's head away.

And Mrs. Rylance turns back to Jordan, I see in the sliver of light closing before me, and puts her arm around him and says, "The *bus*?"

And they laugh and laugh, I can hear, laughing at me and my stutter and my family that takes buses. Laughing clear through my sixteen-floor ride to the lobby, out onto the wet streets, back to Port Authority.

To return home a sopping soldier in tight new clothes.

Returning Home a Sopping Soldier in Tight New Clothes

"Do I have time to stop at Applebee's?"

But I already know her answer.

"No chance. First of all, you're twenty minutes from the bus taking off"—I think Aunt Heidi's saying these words, but she's five feet ahead of me again, jumping over tourists and around strollers, and these are only the approximate consonants and vowels I'm making out above the rain and wind—"and second of all, Applebee's is inedible."

Walking the reverse path to Port Authority, everything that seemed exciting on the way into town now seems frenetic, dangerous, wound up too tight. Maybe because, I dunno, to stop moving so fast might make you realize what an impractical home New York actually is.

Where are the trees in which to hide from your parents?

And when we push past the Montego's sandwich-board advertising man, and I say hi—he did, after all, alert me to the worst outfit I've ever purchased, and that at the very least makes him a unique friend—he doesn't even recognize me, just grunts and shoves another pamphlet into my hand.

"That's a real paper waste," I say to him, "because you already gave me one of these." He probably doesn't recognize me in these tight clothes, and I don't blame him.

"Well, pal," Aunt Heidi says, now standing with me just inside the ancient swinging doors of the bus station. "We should find your gate, and then I have to run. I'm already late."

"For what?" I say, ringing water from my bangs onto the floor.

"Aw Shucks," she says. "Downtown. I'm a hostess at a kitschy oyster place, called Aw Shucks. Which probably sounds gross to a kid."

"It sounds delicious," I say. "I've never had an oyster, and it sounds delicious." The chance to win a pearl; the chance to taste something different than kielbasa or chipped-ham cafeteria sandwiches.

"Well, that's very brave of you. Maybe if you ever make it back to New York, I can make sure you try an oyster. It's kind of a kitschy place"—she already called it that; this must be her routine—"but the food is fresh and we've got great weekend drink specials. There's even a Sunday-night cocktail called The Heidi."

"What does it taste like?" I say.

"Regret and a dusty womb and a *little* splash of orange juice," she says. Heidi's said this to all her friends. Or on first dates, I bet. Bragging about a drink named after her, to somehow justify working at an oyster place instead of following her acting dreams. I just know it.

A group of businesspeople pushes past us, and Heidi says, "Come on, let's move," and after she buys me my ticket home we zoom through the Greyhound bus terminal, passing a Hudson News and an Auntie Anne's Pretzels, a T-shirt shack and a sports-jersey store.

A boy could spend a whole year having fun in a place like this.

"I feel weird putting you on this bus," Aunt Heidi says, likely soaking up the same characters I am.

Exhibit A: Wearing a fur coat and flip-flops and dragging a cat carrying case, a woman next to us is holding a hymnal and will likely want nothing more than to sit next to me and convert me to Christianity by the time we reach Philadelphia.

Who needs an Exhibit B with this kind of Exhibit A?

"Don't worry about it, Aunt Heidi," I say, "I made it here by myself, and I can make it home, too."

Wait! Back up, Nate. A T-shirt stand!

"Can you hold my place in line," I say to Aunt Heidi, "so I can run and get an 'I Heart New York' T-shirt for Libby?" It was all she asked for.

Aunt Heidi looks at her cell phone and sighs. "I'm already late for Aw Shucks, Nate, so run. And be here in two minutes. I'm serious: two minutes. If you don't get on this bus, there's no way you're making it home at a reasonable hour, and I just—this isn't how I want my reunion with your mom to start."

Good. She's considering any kind of reunion at all. This is good.

"Do you have a girl's medium?" I say to the guy at the shack.

"No, boss," the guy says, twiddling a mustache, "only men's medium and men's extra-extra-large." He holds out a T-shirt, black with that signature red heart, and I say, "How much?" and he says, "Thirty dollars."

I gasp. "Thirty *American* dollars?"

And knowing I won't buy it, that I'm just another offended tourist, he goes right back to his cell phone, texting away.

His cell phone. His iPhone. Plugged into a kiosk outlet.

"Sir, sir!" I say, shouting perhaps, from a half foot away. "If I give you, um, ten dollars"—shut up, Nate—"can I, like, throw my phone on your charger for a minute?"

He twists his face at me and says "'Kay, Boss," unplugging his phone and holding out his hand. I burrow into my bag and pull out my ancient iPhone, my bag of money, too, and by the time he's got it plugged in—the familiar chime of a charging phone comforting me—it's been a full five minutes since I left Aunt Heidi.

"Nate!" And here she is. "They are *boarding* your bus and you need to get on, *now*."

"Ten dollars," the man says, holding out his hand, but Heidi yells, "Now!" again, and I unplug my phone and shove it into my pocket (barely; God these jeans are tight). Forget ten bucks. I'm down to single dollars at this point, and I apologize and shuffle back to the line.

I'm the worst friend Libby ever had, though I have the advantage of being the only one she's got, too.

"Sorry about that back there, Aunt Heidi," I say. "I suck."

"You don't suck, you just . . . you are really stubborn, for a kid who's never been outside Pittsburgh."

"How do you know I've never been outside Pittsburgh?" I say.

"Because I know your parents. You've probably—what—only been to Disney, am I right?"

"Yes," I say. Yes, that's exactly right. The woman

in the fur and flip-flops clip-clops by, and I look at her and frown at Aunt Heidi and say, "Well, that was the most exciting and depressing two hours of my life. So: Thank you, for the good parts."

She smiles. "It was really nice to meet you again, Nate. I—I really wish I could see you more often, but you know."

"Yeah," I say. "You wouldn't want to skip town and visit Pennsylvania and miss any shifts at Aw Shucks." She rolls her eyes and holds back a grin. "In case they name a brunch special after you, or something."

"We're shutting these doors, kid," a man calls out from behind us. "Are you on this bus or not?"

"We don't serve brunch," Heidi says, quietly, and gives me a hug, a real one. And just a second later, when she pulls away, her eyes are fully wet, like two of the three rivers that converge at one point in downtown Pittsburgh. And I'd better get on that bus if I want to make it back to Jankburg by nightfall.

Though I've forgotten a single reason to *want* to make it back to Jankburg by nightfall. Or anyfall.

"Bye, Aunt Heidi," I say, tugging my bookbag across the linoleum, waving. "Thanks for the ticket back. And the clothes."

The door shuts, and I'm the very last person on,

which always quickens my pulse. When I'm last on the bus back home, nobody offers to let me sit next to him. I always have to walk with my head down, as quiet as possible, until I find the one kid who's asleep, or a reject himself, and even then I sit with as little of my butt as possible on the very smallest sliver of the very edge of the bus seat, so as not to wake my bus-seat partner.

Here at the Port Authority, I've got the advantage of being the smallest person here *and* the least crazy. A new reason to like New York, all over again—the people may be faster and taller and jugglier and more successful than back home, but it's clear that they're also crazier.

That to immerse myself in their groupings is to emerge the most normal, as well.

I finally decide between the two remaining seats: one next to a regular-enough-looking guy doing a crossword puzzle, but with a giant, Nate-size suitcase placed square atop the seat next to him; or another, next to a grown woman with braids and a doll in her lap, certifiably nuts.

"Would you mind if I sat next to you, sir?"

The crossword guy moves the suitcase to the floor, and I slump into my seat and hug my bookbag. I pull out a mini-donut, and then two more, and then I eat four in all and take a final sip from my water bottle, and then, at last, the bus driver hits reverse and we're off.

And just when I think that the best thing I could do is take a nap, to try my hardest not to cry, to pretend I'm not as wound up as a dreidel (I researched dreidels for the homemade *Fiddler on the Roof* Playbill I created for Libby's mom), my phone flashes a *blink-blink* sound, barely alive from its two minutes of juicing back at the Port Authority kiosk.

I pull it open and, amid the five-thousand logged text messages from Libby and one from Anthony ("You're dead"), an unknown 212 area code has left me a voice mail.

Me.

We break from Port Authority, and the sunlight argues its way through the tinted bus glass, and when I press go on my phone, to listen to the voice mail, this is exactly the message I hear, with _____ signifying the parts that cut out.

"Hi, Anthony, this is _____ from Rex Rollins and Company Casting."

Possibly I pee a little in my pants, here.

"We believe you were just mistakenly _______ but would like _____ at two p.m., today, back at the Ripley-Grier Studios on _____ sixteen. There will be sides ________ and you will need to _______ should expect _______ no later than four or five but please call us _______ hope _____. And be prepared to show us the knee crawl you talked about at the audition."

"Driver!" I yell, practically elbowing the poor crossword guy *(Four-letter word for second chance: N A T E)* next to me. "Stop this vehicle!"

An Outrageous Turn of Events

If I had a pair of scissors, I would cut these jeans off at the knee (after ducking into a private phone booth or an alley; nobody in New York needs to know what kind of underwear I wear). (Hanes Boys, by the way, 'cause whaddo I care if you do.) I'd turn these jeans into shorts and pick up my sprint, en route back to the audition.

I know it doesn't make sense. I know my mom is going to slay me. That Aunt Heidi is heading south (downtown) to Aw Shucks, feeling good about herself, that she finally did *something* resembling conscientious when it came to her nephew or to any child at all.

But there was a mistake made in New York Manhattan City today.

Of course there was a mistake: Garret Charles is practically a million years old and probably misread my number on the audition clipboard, mixing me up with another child! And I'm back in the game. *E.T.* could be mine. I could be the next Elliott.

The first Elliott.

With apologies to Henry Thomas from the movie, who is likely ninety years old now, I bet you.

I text Libby just as my cell phone is powering itself down—"stall. do whatever u need 2 do 2 stall. i got a callback"—but who knows if it goes through. Who cares, even? I may never return to Jankburg now, not unless they're throwing a parade for me.

And I'm out, dashing off the bus, dashing through the terminal, frankly feeling just plain dashing.

There's time for a few buy-or-die errands before I need to be back at that audition, so I pop back to Montego's, like I'm a regular, purchasing a pair of relatively normal-size basketball shorts, on sale for a miraculous single dollar. I'm back on the street and debating, hard, about Applebee's. Aunt Heidi would judge me, but those fajitas are just so darn satisfying. I'm out of dough, besides, and need to replenish my supply. I wonder if Mom has noticed, by now, that her debit card is missing. Usually Dad throws everything on the credit card.

And when I wind my way into a Chase bank—there's two per street, I've noticed, as many Chase banks here as there are Jiffy Lubes back home—and go to take out a hundred dollars (don't worry, I'm paying Mom back with my first paycheck from *E.T.: The Musical: Now on Broadway Forever*), the transaction is denied.

What?

Transaction denied, it says again, when I try a second time. It couldn't be that I've forgotten Mom's pin number. It's just Grandma Flora's birthday, Mom's pin for everything.

"Breathe, Nate," I say out loud, but really I want to be yelling, "*Moose Murders! Moose Murders* it all to tarnation!"

(*Moose Murders*, the most infamous of all Broadway flops and thus reserved as the most critical curse word in the theatrical curse-word canon, ran for exactly one performance on Broadway. One review described a scene in which "a mummified paraplegic rises from his wheelchair to kick a man dressed as a moose in the crotch," according to Wikipedia.)

If the Foster clan doesn't even have a hundred smackers sitting around a crummy Mellon Bank account, not even *E.T.: The Musical* can rescue our finances. We're officially *Moose Murdered*.

I'd plead my case to the bank tellers, maybe even attempting to weep, but I'd probably break into a nervous laugh. Improv is my weakest skill, according to

Libby. I am at my best, as a performer, when playing dead or being fake-punched.

And speaking of performing, let's get on to the audition callback, okay?

You don't need a hundred bucks to audition for a Broadway show; you just need a lucky break. And you can't get that at an ATM.

Moving Ahead: I Know Several Portions of *Hamlet*

"Okay, Anthony Foster"—is this the time to correct them, to finally give my real name?—"you're next. You're on deck."

On deck. This is a term Dad uses with Anthony when they're talking through baseball stuff. "On deck" and then "at bat" and then "steal home." Any minute, Mom'll be wondering when I'm stealing home.

I'm back on the sixteenth floor, the halls now littered not only with us kids auditioning for *E.T.* but a group of women in body stockings and provocative hairstyles (side ponytails, lots of 'em).

This place is like Disney World for adults.

"Anthony!" Oh, boy. "You're up."

Beckany, the ringlet-haired casting assistant whose voice has steadily shredded into a total rasp today, is standing by the door, letting the last child out from her singing audition. The girl isn't exactly crying but is, rather, stunned, as if she's just learned the Tooth Fairy is, in fact, her Uncle Brian or something.

We trade places and I'm through the door, chilly in my new shorts.

The room suddenly feels much bigger, the "creative team" way on the other side, behind a large plastic fold-up table. Mom set out exactly this kind of table in the yard, last summer, for the Celebrate Anthony party (it was just a general celebration for all the trophies he'd won that year).

"And this is Anthony Foster," Beckany says, and when I turn to thank her, she slams the door shut and the lights waver and somebody coughs from behind the desk.

"Hi," I say, bolted to my place.

"Would you like to come out," Rex Rollins says, putting down another can of Diet Coke and licking his fingers of, I believe, hot-wing sauce, "and stand on the little black *x*." He points to the center of the room.

In the time since I was here this morning, they've blocked out the mirrors with a tremendous swath of pink fabric, stretched clear across the room, giving the overall effect that I'm auditioning on a giant tongue.

"Anthony," Rex says—and I'm still not used to responding to this name; I keep expecting somebody to hand me a trophy—"let me reintroduce you to the team." He rolls over and takes me by the shoulder, holding on tight like I'm graduating from high school and he's handing me a diploma. I'm doubtful I'll ever make it through public school alive, so it's kind of nice to get this ritual over with now.

"Oh, no need to reintroduce me, Mr. Rollins," I say, so nervous I can't believe my own moving mouth. "Marc and Mark are the casting assistants"—the two look up from their iPhones, grinning—"and Monica is Mr. Garret Charles's assistant"—Monica waves, her legs up on the table, the kind of gal who seems *thrilled* to be the only girl in the room—"and that, of course, leaves Mr. Garret Charles." Shut up, Nate, shut up, Nate, shut up, Nate.

"Very impressive, Anthony," Rex says, laughing so hard—so over the *top*—that his many chins fold and roll on top of one another, like a big ice cream churner, and threaten to catch my underbite in their tide.

"Oh!" I say, gesturing—put your hand down, Nate. "And let's not forget Sammy!" Sammy, behind the piano, tips a pretends hat and says, "Thanks, kid."

This is either going extremely well—like, they're going to write an entire new role into the show, the Mayor of E.T.'s planet or something, for me—or will go down as one of the great audition disaster stories of all time. Rex Rollins will publish a book: *The Kid*

Who Talked Too Much and Other Cautionary Tales.

A man on the end, clean shaven and somewhere between Mark/Marc's and Mr. Garret Charles's ages, is the only new addition, the only adult here who didn't previously see me almost split my jeans in half. On cue, he smiles at me and says, "Hi, Anthony. I'm Calvin, and I'm the A.D."

My face must change, because Rex Rollins says, "The assistant director, Anthony." He rolls back to behind the desk, asking, "So what will you be singing for us today?"

"I would like to please sing 'Bigger Isn't Better' from the Broadway musical *Barnum*," I say like Libby and I rehearsed, holding my music tight.

"Bring it over here, kid," Sammy says, and I do. "Could you use the piano lid and tap out the tempo you'd like?"

"What do you mean?" I say.

"Just snap for me how quickly you'd like me to play this." Such service! I wonder if Sammy would get me a sandwich, too. I'm starving, never even got a fajita.

Back on my *x* in the middle of the room, I stand there smiling and smiling, smiling so hard my jaw starts to lock, and Sammy calls out, "Let me know when we're ready to go!" and I yell back "Ready!" and he starts.

And perhaps I snapped too quickly.

Suddenly "Bigger Isn't Better"—an adorable song, sung by the little person in a show about circus folk—goes from being a sweet ditty about the merits of being a tiny person to being a warp-speed tongue twister. Words fly from my mouth, just barely, like I'm turning myself in for a murder.

The murder of my own career.

"Oh, gosh," I say, before I've even finished the last verse. "That was terrible. I was terrible."

The room laughs, possibly at me.

"No, it was fine, it was fine," Rex says.

Though I bet you it isn't enough to just be "fine" in New York. *Please*, ladies at *bus* terminals have fur coats, here. "Fine" in New York may be stardom in Jankburg, but it's still just fine.

"Did you prepare a monologue?" Calvin the assistant director says, but maybe not. I can't tell at this point; the sun is high enough now that the table of intimidating people is being backlit, casting them only as a series of judgmental silhouettes. I bet they've never seen a kid in such a tight outfit.

"A monologue?" I say, or stammer.

"Yes," Rex Rollins says, "a short speech from—"

But I want to shout out, "I know what a monologue is, you dip." (I half memorized all seven of Hamlet's speeches last winter, over Christmas break, using them as a prayer before digging into a bucket of KFC.)

"I know several portions of *Hamlet*," I say, and this is the first time bald, British Garret Charles laughs, grunting so hard that the glasses from on top of his head fall, crashing onto a salad. Suddenly I realize the entire team is eating lunch, chomping away like horses at feed.

Mr. Charles leaps up, quickly, in that surprising way an old dancer guy can slink (probably because of his years at the Harry Potter Ballet School or whatever) and changes tactics immediately, his panther jump from the seat turning into the slow, calculated crawl of a turtle. A ticked-off turtle hiding a machete in his shell. "Do you *know*," Garret says, now ten feet away from me, getting closer by the inch, "*when E.T.* takes place?"

"Well, I—"

"1982, Anthony. 1982." I am momentarily pleased that he doesn't know my real name. "1982. And do you know when *Hamlet* takes place, Anthony?" I always assumed, on account of the flowery language, that *Hamlet* took place around 1400, since everything in England takes place in 1400. "1400?" I try, and the table chuckles.

But Garret Charles snaps back at them: *"Enough."* His lip twitches, and he's getting pinker by the insult.

"Not 1400, Anthony. Not 1400 by half." Now he changes the walk entirely, bouncing around me, circling like a werewolf who found a box of sugar. "You know, when I was the movement consultant at the RSC—" He pauses. "Do you know what the RSC stands for?"

"I'm afraid I don't, Mr. Ch—"

"The Royal Shakespeare Company, and if you don't know who Shakespeare is, I don't want to know. The first thing I did, as the movement consultant, was research the period. Get into the head space of these people. For it isn't enough to dance a step—"

And here, Mr. Charles turns on himself, spinning into a double swirl that is, I've got to admit, quite something—like Michael Jackson himself possessed the soul of my old grandpa, including the white socks and black loafers.

"It isn't enough to whip out a fancy turn of footwork—"

And Garret Charles pulls out *another* maneuver, this time marching around like some band leader, pumping his arms, pointing his feet so hard, one of the loafers comes loose and threatens to interrupt his entire interrogation.

I now flick my gaze to the table, catching Monica's billboard-wide eyes.

"The point being," Garret Charles says, "you aren't to come into my temple and waste our time with a *Hamlet* soliloquy when you are, presumably, auditioning for the role of a twelve-year-old boy in 1982 California. *Research* is needed, *research* before submitting any skill to a panel."

"He is," Rex Rollins, now the color of an overripe grape, says, "to be honest, Garret, being considered for a number of tracks."

Garret Charles looks at Rex, wilting him, and then back at me, with a nod to the door. "Unless you've got something appropriate, *age* appropriate and modern and fit for a boy like you . . . Unless you're willing to show us something pleading; for, after all, Elliott's journey is that of a pleading boy, pleading for a father's love, a father we never even meet. Pleading for his new alien best friend not to die on him, not to leave him, throughout the whole of the play."

Libby warned me about people like this. People who refer to musicals as "plays."

Mark and Marc and Rex Rollins are all biting the nails off the fingers of the knuckles they are also cracking. It's my first New York audition and I already know we're going over the time limit, that I've been in here twice as long as the last girl. That Garret Charles has chosen *me* to humiliate, probably to vent his exhaustion at being jet lagged or something.

"So," Garret says, finally wrapping up his own soliloquy, turning from me and pulling a single leaf of lettuce from his salad back on the table, "I'd suggest you collect your music unless you're willing to show us the Elliott side of you." He sits. "Collect your music and head back to mummy."

And then, just like that, something breaks in me, or snaps.

"Funny you should ask about my mom, sir," I shout, and Garret stops whatever he's whispering to Monica, who is, clearly, about to cross my name off her list. "I figured you might do that, figured this might be the first thing you bring up when somebody as little as me—as little *looking* as me—walks up to your Greyhound ticket counter, a counter you're doing one heck of a job manning, to request a ticket out of here. It's downright ludicrous, I'll admit as much, but on the topic of my mom: She's just in the bathroom. And I'm sure she'll be out in just a moment, but she's going through a bit of a stomach ailment and asked that I please take care of my ticket, alone, before she gets out." Mark and Marc stare at me, their jaws collectively dropped to the floor, the grime of a thousand New York auditions blowing into their little bearded mouths. "Because it could take quite a while." And then I *go* for it, risking my worst talent with an improvised, final zinger: "It's a tough thing to have a mom with a stomach ailment, when you barely have a dad at all."

Silence. God, I stink. I need to get back to my

bookbag—where *is* my bookbag—and swipe some deodor—

"Could you take a look at these sides?" Rex Rollins says, creeping over to me like I'm some sort of contagious. "Take a look at script pages one to three, and we'll bring you back in about ten minutes." He hands me a stapled packet of pages, ELLIOTT written across the top.

My face must split into two smiling moons, because Garret Charles stands, skittering the plastic folding table out from underneath the team, and whispers: "Wipe that smile away, Anthony." And I do. "Wipe that smile away and be prepared to keep the attitude of that gift of a monologue you just gave us. *That* is the emotion we are looking for."

"Can I just add," Calvin says, the clean-shaven assistant director at the end of the table, "that you should feel really good about that. That was really nice, Anthony."

"It's N-n-nate, actually," I say, now that I'm getting compliments. "Anthony's just my stage name."

Calvin smiles. "And by the way, what play was your dramatic monologue from, Nate?"

My speech about Mom in the bathroom, cowritten by my best friend. "It's from *Libby Jones Saves the Day*, which is unpublished."

And as Beckany holds the door open for me, handing back my bookbag, Monica shouts out, "When you come back in, make sure your legs are warm. Especially your knees." Garret Charles is beside her, nodding. "We want to see those famous special-skill knee crawls, now that you've got shorts."

And she winks at me just as the door is clicking shut.

Learning Lines

"Does anyone," I say, lugging my bookbag around the hallway, the packet of sides in my hand, "have the time?" And when another little boy looks up from his set of sides and says, "It's a quarter past three," my heart basically jumps out of my throat and beats him up. Or at least that's the look of horror he's giving me, probably in reaction to my own.

Well, it's official.

Mom and Dad are probably leaving the resort now, arguing over who's going to drive home (Mom is the more aggressive driver—we've had to replace the mailbox three times in as many years—but Dad has been known to drive so slowly, you'd think he were double his age).

God, I hope *Dad's* driving them home tonight, wheeling into the side yard sometime between now and the next school year.

I look down at the script. Sides are, according to Libby, selections given to actors at an audition so they don't have to read the whole script.

The little boy with the time, number forty-five, gets called to the audition room, and I watch him take in a library's worth of sheet music, and a hula hoop and a DVD. I must be staring, because his mother leans over to me and says, "That's a video of the duet he sang with Audra McDonald at Carnegie Hall last fall."

"Wow, did he win a contest or something?"

You'd think this lady'd be smiling, but she looks angry or out to prove something, like when Mom comes to me with a broken cereal bowl, or my report card. "No," number forty-five's mother says, "he's just exceptionally talented."

From behind the walls, a tremendous glissando trumps forth from Sammy's piano, and I turn to number forty-five's mom and say, "Wow, what a dramatic audition song. What's he singing?"

"This is how he starts every audition. He's not singing yet. He's playing his recital piece on the piano."

Whoa.

Back to the sides. Stapled, as a cover page, is something called a cast breakdown, with the following:

ELLIOTT - Seeking an ethereal, emotionally intelligent child with an uncommonly clear and beautiful boy soprano voice. Must be comfortable with heights for flying-bike sequence. STARRING ROLE

MICHAEL – ROLE CAST/U.S. ONLY – Elliott's older brother, 16, the quintessential jock. Looking for athletic young adult to play teen. Must be comfortable with heights and driving. Ability to keep close doo-wop harmonies essential. Rock tenor.

GERTIE – Elliott's younger sister, 6 years old. Must stop show cold with "OK, But Where Does This Leave Me?" her plaintive ballad about being stuck as the youngest child in a new household that now includes an alien. Girl soprano.

MARY – Seeking star names (think: country music/Trisha Yearwood era), late 30s to late 40s, Elliott's mother; world weary but a fighter; must exude an Every-mother quality; seeking a thrilling, roaring belt. High alto.

KEYS – ROLE CAST – late 40s to late 60s. Sheriff-type in guise of government agent. Real-butch and not theater-butch; no singing required as of this draft.

GREG, STEVE, and TYLER – MICHAEL's best friends, 16-18. Seeking all ethnicities; must have experience keeping close barber-shop harmonies. All must be comfortable with heights and must "read" high school. A recurring bit includes one of them choking on French fries; commedia dell'arte experience helpful.

ENSEMBLE – tweens to 50s to understudy lead roles and appear in various bits throughout show, from news anchors to students. Must be comfortable with heights; all must be accomplished tap dancers for the finale. Ability to play tuba a plus for female ensemble.

E.T. – the most famous alien of our time; seeking a very small woman or accomplished professional little person performer. Histrionic vocal displays essential.

Gracious me, this packet is thick; I've got less than ten minutes to prepare all the *scenes* and I've barely made it past the character descriptions.

Sweating, I flip the page and see "ELLIOTT, Scene 1" scrawled in photocopied Magic Marker. It looks like Elliott's family is having a pretty boring argument over pizza. Standard set-up. But then? *Drama*.

I live for this stuff.

"*Gertie, did you hear somethin' out back*?" That's Elliott's line, with his brother Michael going, "*Gosh-darned coyotes again, Ma.*"

Man, that's a dynamic exchange. Classic Broadway.

And actually . . . there are a *lot* of dynamic exchanges in this scene. There are a lot of exchanges, period. But forget how *many* words there are; speed-reading ahead, I need to figure out how to deliver stuff like "*we're a crummy family that ain't worth loving*" like a boy. And not a cowboy.

Shaking it off, I sink into a seat and keep studying, diving into scene two. Luckily, this one is just between Elliott and E.T.; I think there's less of a chance I'll be expected to cry in the audition if there's, like, fewer people in the scene. Zooming through the (endless) text, and ignoring my queasy stomach, I land on E.T.'s brilliant last line. "*Gurrrrr gurrrrrrr,*" it goes, with a description just next to it: *Contentment; if a kitten and an apple pie mated, this is what it would sound and smell like.*

Gosh, I *totally* get why Elliott would be friends with E.T.

What I *don't* get is how I'm supposed to memorize all of these pages. Sweet Lord almighty, this is longer than my oral report on irrigation.

And just as I'm starting to read the third sequence

in the packet—lyrics to what looks like Elliott's act two song about getting sicker, called "Whitest Boy Ever," Beckany taps me on the shoulder: "You ready, champ?"

That's nice, at least. The only champ in my life is usually Anthony.

"Oh, I—I was just getting to the third side, and haven't—"

"It's okay," she says, literally lifting me from the wicker hallway chair, "they're only asking people to read sides one and two, anyway, and you're the last kid to go."

And I'm whisked back into the room. Rex Rollins, behind the table, is finishing a hamburger (where did that hamburger come from?) and has moved on to nursing a liter of Diet Pepsi, having now exhausted New York City of its Coke products.

I set my bookbag by the door and slide the rabbit foot deep within my new mesh pockets, keeping it close by for good luck. I'm not particularly superstitious, but I don't like the number thirteen or black cats or opened umbrellas when it's not raining—speaking of which, that storm just won't let up outside—and I'm not afraid to rub a little rabbit for luck. I'll give it one more chance.

"Okay, Nate," Rex says, "let's just take a quick look at side number one, and then we can be on our way." Actual bits of hamburger meat cascade from his mouth. Sammy is closing the lid to the piano and putting his jacket on, and, if I'm not mistaken, beginning to open his umbrella.

"Okay. Thank you," I say, stopping to cough, "thank you for seeing me today, and I just want to warn you that I haven't memorized these wonderful scenes yet."

Mark and Marc, organizing piles of headshots behind the table, giggle for some reason.

"No need to memorize those sides, Nate," Rex says. "Just go ahead when you're—"

But I'm so excited that I cut him off, starting in on Elliott's lines, working my way down the whole page.

"Gertie, did you hear somethin' out back?" I turn and look to the door, deciding to make the Ripley-Grier hallway the "out back" of Elliott's house in the script.

"No, sir," I say as Gertie, pitching my voice into a lispy soprano, licking my fingers since she's supposed to be "eating pizza" according to the sides.

For some reason Marc and Mark laugh harder now, and my eyes flit up to them. I simultaneously scold myself (an actor must *never* break the fourth wall and look at the audience, which I'm always hounding Libby about) and launch right back in: sticking my chest out, sitting into my left hip, putting on the persona of my mom, who is a distinctly perfect model for the role of Mary, Elliott's mom.

"Elliott," I say, wagging my finger at the air, *"finish*

your dinner. I mean it." I whip around and reassume the role of Elliott. *"I just coulda sworn I heard a rustling in the garbage cans. I bet Michael didn't put 'em away, neither."* God I hate that line.

I squint for two seconds and channel Anthony—"16, the quintessential jock"—basically he *is* Michael. *"Gosh-darn coyotes again, Ma,"* I say, yawning, scratching my armpits. Anthony is always scratching his armpits.

"Watch your mouth, Michael," I say, wringing my hands and sighing a lot. Mom always does those things when she's staring out the window.

Garret Charles grunts, here, I think.

"Mom," I say, heading to the door of the audition room, *"I'm going to the bathroom. Make sure the dog doesn't get to my plate."*

I glance at the page—I guess I'd memorized more of this than I realized—and drop to the floor, spinning around on my butt. *"Plate, mate, fate, plate,"* I say as Gertie, biting my lips, gurgling, playing not so much Elliott's adorable younger sister but, like, an idiot monkey starved of nutrients. I think I might even pretend to pick an ant from my hair and eat it, but who can tell, the whole thing is going so fast.

At this point, the room is roaring. I can see out of the corner of my eye that Sammy has taken his coat off and is texting somebody furiously. Rex is waving his arms at me, but I can't stop. My mouth is like a marble rolling down a hill.

"Stupid girl," I say, jumping to my feet and loping around like a caveman. Like Anthony. *"Rhyming all day long."*

"Watch your mouth, Michael," and my voice cracks on *mouth*, a big over-the-top Mom-about-to-cry crack. And, my God, Calvin the assistant director is scribbling something on his notepad at the table.

"Would everybody just stop fighting," I yell, standing by the audition door.

And then I remember a theory that *I* actually taught *Libby*: "Play the opposite."

If a scene calls for screaming, don't scream. When we did our basement workshop on *Les Misérables*, Libby studied the role of Eponine, and I made her practice the entire song, "A Little Fall of Rain," as if it werc the smiliest lullaby you ever heard. It's actually about a young girl who gets shot in a war and is dying in the arms of her really hot friend, but if you smile through such a tragedy, it disarms the audience. Freaks them out. Makes them think you're a little crazy.

Makes them keep looking at you.

"A little crazy," I explained to Libby that day, "is a lot more interesting to watch than a girl who's been shot."

So I channel that day—that day of getting quiet

when you're supposed to be loud; about grinning when you get shot—and decide to read Elliott's final monologue with jabs of crazy-person laughter, belying his breakdown at the dinner table.

"It's enough—mwa-hahaha—*that a kid can barely keep his thoughts straight. You—picking on our sister all day*—hahahaha!—*and you, Ma"*—and I whisper this part—*"waiting by the door for Pa to come home. Well, he's not!" That* part I yell. You've got to yell *sometimes.*

The last line is *"He's not, because we're a crummy family that ain't worth loving,"* but that sounds like something from *Little House on the Prairie* or whatever. It doesn't live up to *E.T.* It's just not good enough. So I go for broke and rewrite on the spot.

"Dad's not coming back because we're not worth it. Because this is a house full of people, sure, but empty of anything worth loving. Especially me," I say real slow, and then turn on myself, and open the door. And slam it shut behind me.

Because there's only two ways to treat a door in a scene: Slam it shut or fling it open. The rest is amateur.

I take a deep breath in the hall, and then, glancing down again at the sides, blurry on account of my rapid-fire hand shuddering, make out the older brother's last line of the script page. I shout through a crack in the door (in a stupid southern drawl—*who* knows why): *"The bathroom's the other way, turtle-brains. That's out back to the yard!"*

Three more quick breaths, and then a slow one.

"Are *you* reading for the role of Michael?" a boy asks, and I turn to see Jordan Rylance sitting outside the door.

"No, I"—my voice is hoarse, battered at the edges, and my hand not holding the sides is still glued to the doorknob. "I just read all the parts to side number one. Because they gave me all the lines."

On cue, the hallway around me bursts into laughter. The mean kind. The you've-got-toilet-paper-on-your-shoe kind.

I look back at the door and turn the knob, but it won't budge. I'm locked out. My bookbag is inside, and my donuts and pride and dreams, too.

At once it swings back, knocking me over almost, and Rex Rollins looks me in the eye and is full of some kind of unreadable expression. Like he's just been crying or throwing up.

"Nate," he says, quiet, "could you calmly walk back into the room?"

"Nate!" Calvin the assistant director says, standing to greet me. "Come on back. That was really something."

Everyone else is still sitting at the table, eyeing me like I might burst into flame.

I walk back to the *x*. "Would you mind, ladies and sirs"—shut up, Nate—"giving me one more shot at side number one? Because I swear I won't slip into a stupid southern accent on the Michael lines again."

"That won't be necessary," Garret Charles says. I thought he was just the dance guy, but he sure has a lot to say about acting. I guess all British people are experts on acting and accents and scene-work and dramatic structure, or something.

"Nate, how tall are you?" Rex Rollins says.

"On your knees," Garret says. "How tall are you when gliding across the floors on your knees, and are we ready to show that particular trick?"

But by the time he has said the words "are we ready," I'm circling their table, channeling my *Fiddler on the Roof* bottle dancing, flying by like we're at a racetrack, the team's little greyhound.

Greyhound.

Buses.

Mom is going to kill me for all of this.

"Good God," Monica says, by now having leapt upon Sammy's piano lid. "Could I tie a towel to your knees and would you come over and mop my apartment?" This gets a big laugh from the team, so I yuk-yuk right alongside them and possibly even slap my knee.

I leap up, back to the *x*, and say, "I was able to

do that, two shows a day, for a whole weekend of performances in my friend's basement back home." But, actually, I'm gasping between each word, so it's breathier than that.

"Nate, are you visiting town for the first time?" Calvin says. I wonder what he's getting at.

"Well, I mean, technically yes, but I feel like a native already. The—uh—the A train was running local this morning, and it really ticked me off."

Calvin smiles again, the inverse reaction to Garret Charles (who rolls his eyes so hugely, I think he's either having a stroke or doing a corneal impression of the setting sun), and says, "Will you be around for a few days is what I meant."

Holy cow!

"Absolutely," I say, or scream. "Absolutely I'll be around for a few days." Since Mom and Dad have probably rented my room out already, or Anthony has turned it into a free-weight studio, I'm practically not even lying.

Sammy stands from behind the piano and says, "Can I just make a note about something, Nate? What's your top note?"

My top note? Vocally? I always crack on the bridge of "And I Am Telling You I'm Not Going" (the Jennifer Holliday version, not the movie—as if).

"Jeez, I'm not exactly sure. I'm a—uh—'boy

soprano with a gutsy chest voice,' according to my best friend."

Sammy looks at the team, and his eyes go wide: "I think I'm going to Tweet that later on." Though I might have misheard him.

A knock from behind me, and I turn to see a short man duck his head in and say, "We got this studio now, folks," and Rex says, "Just one second, sir, I promise we're just on our way."

The whole team stands on cue, desperate for some fresh, wet air, I presume. Rex Rollins walks up to me and says, "Well, nice job today, Nate, and welcome to New York." And all those crazy quirks about his face, the rolling chin and sweaty forehead, they melt away. And he just about looks like Santa Claus after a close shave.

"Thank you, Mr. Rollins," I say, and when Marc, the sassier of the two bearded boys, opens the door to let me out, and I turn to thank the rest of the team, they're all hunched over the desk, chatting loudly. Marc says, "You see that girl in the corner, the one with the long hair?"

And indeed, there she is, a new girl I hadn't even noticed, sitting in a metal fold-up chair and looking at her iPhone.

"That girl," Marc says, "is the *reader*. And her job is to read all the parts on the page that *aren't* your part." Oh, God. "So you were really *just* supposed to be reading Elliott." He's gaining volume and kind of enjoying ridiculing me, the way somebody just a few years older than you can love power more than genuinely old people like your parents.

"Though"—a voice sneaks up, and Calvin pops out from behind Marc's shoulder—"your best friend is right. You're definitely gutsy, buddy." He pats me on the head and says, "Nice to meet you, Natey Foster."

And I decide that Natey Foster is a better stage name than Anthony Foster anyway, a better stage name all along. Especially if I can learn to say it without a stutter.

I'm floating back to the elevator bank, my limbs and bookbag and good-luck rabbit foot drifting around me as if suspended in the syrupy ooze of celebration. And as I turn the corner, past the Vitamin Water display, Marc comes running after me.

"Nate," Marc says, suddenly in a nice voice. He's not out of breath at all, and probably spends most of his life in the gym on account of his rippling biceps, not that a kid like me would notice them. "Could you just come back to the room, for one more second?"

"Did I leave something in there?" I ask, following him back.

"The team just wants to talk to you."

Usually when groups of adults want to speak to

me it's because a grandparent has died or I've let Feather pee on somebody's flower bed.

"Nate!" they all say when I walk through the door.

"Yes?" I say back, or yell, or scream.

"We can't stop talking about you," one of them says. "We've never seen an audition like yours." At this point, forgive me, the dizziness of the day has taken such a toll, I'm not even sure whose mouth is moving. I'm not even sure if it's a person talking, and not my dreams.

"I hope that's a good thing," I say, and can feel my leg shaking.

"Well, it's always good to be memorable," Garret Charles says, "though we can't figure out what *makes* you so memorable." He appears to now be wearing all *three* pairs of his glasses. Man, he must be old.

I turn to the side, right here on the centered *x*, and point at my mouth: "Usually it's the underbite. My most memorable feature is my underbite, and it goes down from there, literally."

"Nate," Rex Rollins says, "is this cell phone number, here, on your application sheet—is this the best number to call you?"

"Absolutely sir," I say, or maybe shout or sing.

"Okay, well, as long as you're in New York anyway, we may want to see you again. For a callback. So just . . . stand by."

Stand by, indeed.

Calvin gets up again. So far, he's my best friend here, tall and footbally but with none of the football vibe I've come to associate with guys who look like him. He doesn't seem to want to beat me up at all.

"Hey, and Nate," he says, opening the door, showing me to the hallway for the hundredth time today. "Don't be afraid to put a little more deodorant on. You know? It's something every guy goes through, and it's probably time for you as well."

Nobody in my family would ever have given me such simple, helpful advice.

Anthony would have wrapped it in a lecture on how it wouldn't matter even if I *didn't* stink, because no girl would want to come near me in a million years. And Dad wouldn't have even noticed me, himself smelling like janitor fumes (equal parts Lysol and banana peels, like a comedy act gone horribly clean). And Mom? Well, Mom can never have a tough talk with me, passing it all off to Dad, who passes it all off to God. Mom just talks in figure eights, making everything around her dizzy.

"Honest, Nate," Calvin says, "I have to put on my Mitchum three times a day in the summer, sometimes." (*Mitchum!* So much for the store-brand stuff that I packed.) "Wait'll *you* survive a New York summer."

And he hands me a ten-dollar bill.

With that, I'm drifting back down the hall, out to the street, off to Duane Reade, floating and stinking and smiling, off to the Mitchum deodorant aisle, a grown-up in New York City.

Not only alive, by God, but thriving.

Starmites My Life to Oblivion

And starving. Thriving and starving and stinking broke (and stinking *stinking*) and without a place to sleep. Oh my God, it's gotten superdark out, too, superfast. How did I not plan for this?

What would the character Elliott do?

E.T. would probably build Elliott a fort out of Reese's Pieces, or something.

That settles it.

I'll pick up some Reese's Pieces en route to the Mitchum deodorant aisle, as inspiration. Plus, Reese's are loaded with protein (peanut butter is a complex protein, according to the parts of my Health class I didn't practice my autograph during), and I've got to get something to eat. Anything at this point.

It's five o'clock, and this Duane Reade across from Port Authority, brightly lit and practically cheerful, might be the nicest drugstore I've ever visited, decorated with cutouts of ghosts and goblins: something that might've scared me even just a few years ago, when I was a kid.

I've got ten dollars, exactly, ten dollars and one penny to stretch between candy corn (starch), Reese's Pieces (protein), and, critically, Mitchum (pride).

Also, I should figure out where I'm going to sleep tonight. Yeah, that.

Starmites! Where am I going to sleep? (1989; sixty performances; the musical's setting was a place called Shreikwood Forest, and I'm not kidding.)

Starmites my life to oblivion.

And as I break into my version of a mild panic (lightly humming the evacuation scene from *Miss Saigon* in an unreasonably high key), I get the first good idea in all of this trip. The Duane Reade travel aisle is awash in everything a kid like me would need: tweezers (never underestimate the power of tweezers) and mini-deodorants and mouthwash and—this is the exciting part—an entire bin full of cell-phone chargers.

I drop to my knees and rummage through, finally landing upon my beloved/hated iPhone plug-in. It's $4.99, on sale, and that should leave enough change for one more item: I go with Reese's Pieces, figuring food is more important than my stench right now and that I can take care of all that by giving myself a good scrub-down later on tonight.

In the bathroom of wherever I . . . uh . . . end up.

Starmites.

"Would you like to make a donation to children with cerebral palsy?" the salesperson says, scanning my items. I'm actually kind of glad I'm not buying my new Mitchum, because a girl would be embarrassing to buy deodorant in front of. It's like how I can't figure out how *any* adult buys toilet paper with a straight face.

"Sorry, I can't afford it," I say, "but would you like to make a donation to children who don't have a place to sleep tonight?"

She doesn't laugh.

I make for the exit, and in the city wind I'm an instant icicle, a Nate-pop, and duck back into the store to throw my jeans on over my flag-size shorts. This is like trying to stuff overbaggy boxers into a pair of tight pants. I don't know how Anthony does it. This is the chief reason I wear tighty-whities.

Then I do something really bad, and I'm just going to fully disclose it here because I can edit it out later. Sitting just by the drugstore exit, a box teems with donated winter coats.

A Winter Coat drive.

Everything is extreme here. Winter doesn't really start back home, not on the clock anyway, until mid-November. I guess in Manhattan you have to start putting on winter coats early in the season, so you don't freeze on your walk between Duane Reade and the cardboard box you'll eventually sleep in tonight.

"I'll just Google this charity and donate my first week of *E.T.* salary to it," I say out loud. And when I finally find a winter coat I like—a big hood trimmed with fake fur, and a cool crisscross of electric yellow and burgundy—a security guard from Duane Reade appears like a ghost. I throw on the jacket and dash out onto Forty-second Street, smacking straight into a pretzel cart and a woman with a stroller and a guy on a scooter and a couple other kids.

I smack into a lot of things pretty regularly, actually.

Luckily, the jacket is about thirty sizes too big for me, shielding me from trauma. God, if I get sent back to General Thomas Junior High, I should just wear this all day long: a padded bruise protector.

I bruise easily.

I've got to eat something.

And when I pull my furry yellow hood back, a blazingly huge Chevys, the biggest and most wholesome Mexican restaurant in America and likely the world, is draped across the sky like a billboard tailored to my heart.

And I've got a plan.

A Salsa Crawl Is Not a Dance Move

"Table for two, please," I say. "My mom is *just* about to show up. And preferably we'd like something by the door."

The nice-enough lady walks me clear to the other side of Chevys (not by the door at all) and seats me beneath a hanging potted plant, confirming my theory: Everything green in New York is potted. An island of asphalt is simply not fit for growing things. I find that so inspiring.

"Oh!" I say, just as she's clearing a table for me. "Do you have something with a plug? I don't even need a view of Times Square or anything, but an outlet is crucial."

She kind of puffs her cheeks out, like she's dealing with another stupid out-of-towner (which, to be honest), and seats me all the way upstairs, right by the bathroom. Not ideal for a number of reasons (the combo of bathroom smells and salsa, chiefly) *and* it'll make my eventual escape tougher, but by golly there's a plug right beneath the booth.

In thirty seconds, my phone is back in business.

I won't bore you with the texts that have filed in; there are roughly a trillion, most from Libby, a few from Anthony, and one from . . . oh, God. Mom.

"WE ARE WORRIED SICK WHERE R U NATHAN."

Whenever Mom texts, it's serious. She's as averse to technology as I am to pencils.

Oh, God. Oh, God. Oh, God.

And to make things worse, I can't even counterbalance the narrative by providing an encouraging message from Rex Rollins the casting director, because the only *voice mails* are from Mom, too (same all-caps message as above, with more shrieks, and my dad stomping around in the background), and one from Libby: "Call me ASAP, Jack."

"Can I get you anything to drink?" a new voice says.

My head jerks up, poking out from its furry yellow hood, my elbows barely reaching the table. This berserk-looking Ewok is starving. "A water with a lemon and a lime both, please, and the largest free basket of chips that you're allowed to bring me."

The waiter smiles and kind of glides away. The

good news is, I have my protein/dessert already taken care of (shout-out to Mr. Reese: love your Pieces, sir), and the dual serving of fruit slices in the water checks *that* box off the list. Plus, the chips and salsa are like a free, cold pizza, which happens to be my favorite way to eat piz—

What am I doing? I have to call Libby.

Two rings and she picks up.

"Libby!"

"Hi—uh—*Mom*," she says in her "acting" voice.

Uh-oh. Trouble.

"Stay with me," she mutters into her phone, and I make out a series of slams and yells and the general hubbubery of angry adults in the background.

And too many men's voices.

There are no men's voices in Libby's house, unless she's listening to the cast album of *Damn Yankees*. And even then it would sound more like a gentle baseball game and less like . . . this.

The waiter brings my water and basket of chips, placing a glorious salsa bowl in front of me, and I put my hand to the receiver and whisper to him: "Allow me to mull over the menu until my mom gets here, please," and I'm back to my bestie. "What's going *on*, Libby?"

"You tell *me*," she says.

"Well, the stats: I'm at a Chevys in Times Square."

"You're still in *New York*?" she says in a stage whisper.

"Where are *you*?"

"At *your* house, along with half the neighborhood, and your parents. Your mom is, like, threatening to call the police."

"The *police*?" I say, or yelp. The people at the table next to me, a bunch of tourists (in coats that fit them), stop eating and stare at me.

"I know. It's dramatic. But you *are* the very definition of a missing minor at this point."

I would stand and pace but don't want to unplug the phone from its socket. Gosh these chips are good, at least. Chips just work on every level, you know?

"So what—gosh, what am I going to do?" I say.

"Uh—get on the next *bus*?"

I'd meant that question rhetorically. I don't like Libby taking this tone with me. It's very Mama Rose/ Gypsy, and I'd never be comfortable playing a stripper.

"The audition actually went very *well*, Libby. *By the way*. Like: I didn't get cut, or I did at first but then got called back."

"You got a *call*back?" she shrieks, and then I hear her turn from the phone and say, "It's nothing, Mrs. Foster. My mom is just checking on me."

Feather barks and this just about breaks my heart, so in tribute I break a chip in half and eat it without my hands, just like he would.

"Yup. I mean, I sang for the team today and everything."

"The *team*," Libby says, chuckling. "You are so boss, Nate. You are boss."

I'm boss! This is Libby's greatest compliment! Usually *she's* boss and I'm not even vice boss.

"So what now?" she says, and I swear I hear our grass crunching beneath her feet, Libby walking out her worries so that I don't have to.

"Well, I'm doing a salsa crawl, starting with Chevys. Because I'm broke. Like, I have no idea where I'm going to sleep tonight."

"I can Google 'youth hostels.' I didn't think it would come to this, but I can do some work on that. Also, my mom has that step-brother who lives in Queens."

"Interesting," I say. "But how do you get to Queens? Do I have to charter a bus or something?"

"Prob'ly," Libby says. "The only thing I really know about New York is what's playing on Broadway, y'know? Did you read they're doing a revival of *Into the Woods* where all the actors play their own instruments?"

"Coolio." The waiter returns. "Could you tell me what you have on, like, special, sir?" I say, crooking my head against the phone, which is still partially concealed by my hood, and pretending to listen to him. Libby and I just have so much to catch up on. "Keep talking," I ventriloquize to her.

"Okay," she says, launching. "So here's the thing: There's a Nate Foster neighborhood watch and everything. The Kruehler family is patrolling the front of the cul-de-sac, and your dad is on the roof with a big flashlight. And somebody went to school, suggesting—this was actually hilarious—that you might have gone in to the library, on a *Sunday*, to study."

That *is* hilarious, hilarious and sad.

" . . . and we've got a chimichanga that people are really responding to," the waiter says, finishing up a pitch that he *really* oversold. His teeth are so white that he must be an actor.

"Thank you," I say to him, waving the empty basket of chips in the hopes he catches my drift for a refill. "Let me pray on those dinner specials over another basket of chips. Carl."

(I caught his name tag. Always good to address people by their names.)

"Nate, I'm really proud of you," Libby says. "You not only made it to New York, you seem to be taking advantage of every loophole I ever taught you."

Carl returns with the basket of chips and another water (with only one lemon and *no* lime, which'll make me feel better when I don't order anything, or tip him) and I say, "My mom should be here any moment, Carl, just bear with me," and he does a theatrical double-eyebrow bop and glides away to another table.

"The thing I can't figure out, Libby, is why Anthony hasn't sold me out."

"Well, that's the thing. In your absence, without the distraction of scene-studies and showtunes, I've gotten more self-reliant. One could say 'resourceful.'" She sounds dangerous right now, but the fun kind.

"What *kind* of resourceful?" I say, swallowing seven chips at a time and licking a finger.

"There was an incident in your brother's room," Libby says, or huffs actually. She's climbing up our favorite tree out back, I'm just sure.

"Yes—was this the thing where you were in Anthony's underwear drawer?"

"You *know* about that?" she says, squealing, probably almost losing her grip on the tricky third branch from the top.

"Yes, my Aunt Heidi informed me. Anthony called her and spilled the beans, and she found me at the audition—which *you* must have told him about—and now I'm here. Though she doesn't know it. You and me and my waiter Carl are the only people who even know I'm in New York, Libby." He's back. "Carl!"

"Mister Kid, is your mom ever arriving?"

"I'm hoping so. Yeah, she's just down the block at

Applebee's, comparing appetizer pricing"—I can hear Libby sigh, probably marveling at how much sharper my improv skills have gotten since moving to New York—"but should be here any minute."

Carl glides away again. Gosh his sideburns are manicured; it's really something.

"Okay. So, Nate, I have to run in a second or it's going to look suspicious to your parents. But I never approved an overnight." The wind is picking up in Jankburg, and I can barely hear her. "This trip was to be a bus ride there and a bus ride back, with one hour popping your head into an audition and an important stop at a T-shirt stand, for me."

"I know, I really trie—"

"We don't have time for explanations."

"You mean like *what you were doing in my brother's underwear drawer*?"

"Okay, let's talk about that. Okay, I was curious what the great star Anthony Foster wears underneath his jerseys."

"And pole vault uniform and soccer shorts and—"

"Yes, exactly. But you don't know the good part, because I'm sure he didn't tell your Aunt Heidi *this*." She pauses. Plays the opposite, just like I taught her. "I found *beer* in your brother's sock drawer."

"What?!" If I were on the tree next to Libby, I'd have fallen into the yard below.

"Yeah, a full-on six-pack of Iron City. And he had nothing to say. *You* know what your parents would do if they knew he was drinking."

I *do* know.

"All he's saying to your parents, and the police, is that you went to my house for a sleepover and he hasn't heard from you since. It doesn't help, Nate, that you took the lucky rabbit foot."

I'm rubbing it now, actually. Have been rubbing it since that audition, one hand stealing winter coats and eating chips, and the other, it turns out, not letting go of that rabbit foot.

"Because," she says, "everyone knows you don't go anywhere important without that rabbit foot, and that you wouldn't have taken it with you for a regular old overnight at your girl Libby's."

Usually it hangs on a hook by my bed, my version of a dream-catcher. Libby's right; it is totally suspicious that the rabbit foot is missing from my room.

"So your parents showed up at *my* house tonight, and luckily my mom was asleep, and there I was, on my bed, doing a jigsaw puzzle of the Mona Lisa, and *in* barge your mom and dad." The Joneses never lock their doors.

"My God, even my dad showed up?" I say. For me?

"Yes. Like, evidently one second after Anthony

lied and said that you were at my house, they arrived here. So you know it was your *mom* who drove them over."

Carl the waiter is finishing up with a table across the way; I don't have any more stall time. I'm up, unplugging the charger, and stuffing it into one of my wondercoat's many pockets.

I bolt into the men's room, whispering: "So what did you say to my parents?"

"That we're playing an elaborate new-generation version of hide-and-seek where you get twelve hours to find a hiding space, anywhere in the neighborhood. And that it was your turn to hide."

"Goodness," I say, ducking into a Chevys bathroom stall. "And they bought it?"

"Yeah," Libby says, yawning, "I did the crying thing."

"Of course."

"So you have until tomorrow morning to get back home, Nate, before, like, the FBI is involved. The whole thing is actually *like E.T.*, all these guys running around looking for you in the woods."

I have another Reese's Piece. "It's not going to happen." My voice echoes off the tile. "Me getting home tomorrow morning? I'm supposed to be on standby here; the casting people told me I might be getting a call to come back in or something."

"Holy *Gone with the Wind*, Nate. Honest. This is so boss."

"Libby, even *I* know *Gone with the Wind* was a monumental hit, even if it's unwatchable now."

"Not the movie, wise guy. There was a London musical of the same name, but it played when we were little. I wouldn't expect you to know about any musical flop created before you met me. But, yeah. Huge-ol' floperoo."

I pee and finish up and practically scream when I catch sight of myself in the mirror, thinking I'm actually a small man sneaking up behind myself to murder me in the Times Square Chevys. Turns out a bright yellow and burgundy jacket can be quite an intimidating combo.

"So where are you *staying* tonight, then?" Libby says. "Let's figure this out."

I exit the bathroom. "My Aunt Heidi's address is listed in Mom's book in the kitchen. I can crash at her place, maybe. Definitely."

"Too dangerous," Libby says. "Much too. There are a thousand grown-ups in your kitchen"—I can practically hear her squinting to see across the lawn—"and one of the Kruehler boys is having an arm-wrestling competition with your brother, and—oh! Anthony's winning."

"Libby, stay with me."

"Sorry. Any other ideas?"

I see an exit sign at the end of the bathroom hallway and make a hard left, passing a waitress holding a tray of calamari.

Of *course*.

"I have an idea, Libby." How did I not think of this before? "Can you get in front of a computer?"

"Hmm, depends on if your dad finally broke down and got your family one, now that you've run away. Like, now your house can be officially fun."

"He didn't, I can assure you. I need you to run back to your place. Say you have to check on your mom. Run home and text me the address of something called Aw Shucks. It's an oyster place downtown."

"Oh, that's cute, the play on shucks," Libby says with some effort, clearly swinging her leg over the biggest trunk, climbing back down our tree.

"Watch that third branch," I say, but she says, "Ow," and then, "Too late," and I hear her land in the yard.

"I have to hand it to you, Mom," she's saying to *me*, I guess—lying in front of the adults, sliding open our broken screen door and walking back into my house, everyone probably staring at her—"you're really brave. You really are the bravest person I know."

And she hangs up and probably starts to wail again for everyone, and I break through the Chevys back-staircase street exit just as Libby is probably skipping home.

Leaping over bushes as I leap potholes.

Passing stray dogs as I do clusters of garbage.

Each of us on our own journey tonight, in honor of me.

A neighborhood that never cared about me before, suddenly spinning into itself, looking everywhere but here.

A whole world revolving around Nate Foster, for once.

It's practically embarrassing.

Practically.

Accepting Saviors

Momentarily full from chips and salsa—almost too full; I could regret this later—I'm back outside, making my way downtown, back toward the Ripley-Grier audition studios. It's a flying guess that south is generally heading toward Aunt Heidi's restaurant.

At any moment, Rex Rollins the casting director could call, so I'm clutching my dying phone in one hand and, no doubt about it, that lucky rabbit foot in the other. I probably look a little like Mom when she goes mall walking and takes along those silly purple three-pound weights, her double-fisted hands a-swinging.

She would throw those weights at my head, right now, if she saw where I was.

There goes Madison Square Garden again, and with it—with any arena, anywhere—an ocean of Anthony floods over me. Anthony the star? Him I know. Anthony with a calf tear? Anthony the beer drinker? There is so much about my brother that's undiscovered, I guess, and not just what he sees in that high school girlfriend of his, with the tight sweaters and overreliance on Bubble Yum as a leading personality trait.

I pass a giant post office, across from Madison Square Garden, its mammoth stairway straight out of that triumphant scene in *Rocky* (Dad made me watch it once, hoping it'd butch me up; instead I cried throughout and referred to myself as "the Adrian of our family" for the rest of that week).

Next, a sign, taped haphazardly to an upcoming light pole, promises SOULS SAVED AND A FREE WAFFLE at some church in Harlem. Whoops. Happened this morning. There went my chance at a free waffle. And a saved soul.

And I'm taken back to the last time Anthony and I were anything even close to close.

He and I went away to a Christian camp, at Dad's insistence: Youth Truth 'n Spirit, up in the Poconos Mountains. It was a thrill, Mom allowing us out of the house for more than a sleepover, allowing us farther than twenty minutes outside Jankburg. We loaded up on buses and it was the best day of my life, riding alongside *the* Anthony Foster, who was, even at thirteen—gosh, my age now—a budding community mascot, raising money for the kids' library fund, having sports scholarships named after him.

Anthony and I shared earbud jacks, and he picked the whole soundtrack, narrating our ride up to the mountains with cool, older-kid music: Wilco and Santogold and Vampire Weekend, bands that I'd never even heard of, let alone played myself. I didn't submit a single entry to our improvised playlist, because I wasn't old enough to have an iPod and I only listened to Disney soundtracks at the time, besides.

This was pre-Libby, pre-showtune, pre-anything that I now look to as my true religion. Before she moved to Jankburg and changed my life.

Anthony and I got to the Poconos and bunked together, and he accepted Jesus Christ as his savior that weekend. And I *thought* I did, too, but I think I was just so wrapped up in the spectacle of it all—all the older boys playing acoustic guitar with their shirts off, for one; and the camp counselors dressing up as the Devil to scare us at midnight—that emotion overcame me, and I concluded that that feeling must have been Jesus. That maybe knowing Jesus was like crying and making new friends and being scared and not having parents around, all at once.

I stood onstage and declared my new Christianity, in front of hundreds of other kids. (Other than *Vegetables: Just Do It*, when I understudied the legumes, it was the first and last time I'd ever been on a stage, actually). The setting was this hollow outdoor bandshell, with Christian fireflies lighting the non-Christian tears on my face a shocking blue (somebody posted photos on Instagram, after). And I took a microphone and yelled out, "My name is N-n-nate F-f-foster, and this weekend I accepted Jesus Christ as my savior."

I thought it would make me belong, somehow. To a club. Any club. Any club that would have Nate Foster as a member.

And that night, having just welcomed Jesus Christ into my regular cast of characters, I got beat up outside the camp cafeteria by Larry Motlie and his Motlie Crew (all of my bullies have great gang names), who politely informed me that "God hates fags." Even though I had nothing against God, and wasn't even—and am not even, now—sure what I was.

And when I got back to our bunk, Anthony was sitting in a circle with a bunch of other boys. They were reciting Bible verses aloud, and I was so embarrassed at my own bleeding lip, at my own swollen-shut eye, that I immediately doubled back out into the community yard, before any of them saw me, and put a brown paper bag, from the garbage can outside the cement bunk, over my head. And pretended to come in and spook them. Pretended to be a ghost.

I just didn't want anyone to see my face.

And Anthony leapt up and pushed me into the wall and told me I wasn't being a very good soldier of Christ. And I hadn't even taken the bag off. He just knew it was me. My underbite was probably jutting out.

I rinsed off in the group showers—thank (my complicated friend) God nobody was in there—and winced through the physical pain of all that tepid camp water splashing into my bleeding gums; delighted, still, that none of my brother's bunk friends had to see my secret that night. That even with God on my side, everyone still hated me. I still wasn't fast enough, not with an answer in Social Studies, not on the field with a football. I was still the kid who threw up back home on Tuesday nights, knowing Wednesdays were Shirts and Skins day in P.E., and what if I had to be Skins? And take my shirt off in front of the other boys? That even with God as a friend, I was still broken.

And on the bus ride back to Jankburg, Anthony must've sensed that I'd dropped the God routine as fast as I'd adopted it. And he didn't let me sit next to him. I had to sit with the adult chaperone who smelled like Funyons.

And now, under this New York sky where nobody knows my name, I'm passing my fourth (fourth!) cupcake shop (if you've never been to New York, there are, I can report as an eyewitness, entire shops devoted *only to cupcakes*, and you can find these shops spaced about twenty feet apart splaying out into every direction). I never want to go home. I never want to ride another bus again, or see Anthony, or accept Jesus Christ as my personal anything.

My phone rings.

"Jesus Christ!" I yell, jumping, knocking into a *Village Voice* canister.

"It's me."

"Hi, Lib."

"Where are you now? And I've only got a minute, because I need to patrol your house and make sure the cops never actually came."

"Goodness, this is serious. Okay, I'm—let's see—I'm in front of a really weird building that looks like a 3D triangle, or something."

"Be more specific, Nate," Libby says, clicking away at her computer. She's so lucky. Her family has *two* computers, and Libby has her own, even.

"Well, to my left is a sliver of a park, like somebody's yard in Jankburg, but I'm sure this is considered, I dunno, maybe The Central Park?"

"If you're at Central Park we're officially *Flora, the Red Menace*-d," Libby says.

I don't know that flop, and make a note to look it up if I survive the night; at least three people have already looked like muggers to me, though one of them was holding hands with another guy, which was kind of interesting.

"Okay, the street sign—let's see—it looks like I'm at the point of Twenty-third and Fifth Avenue streets."

"Oh!" Libby says, typing madly. "Wait! I think you're at . . . the . . . Flatiron Building, it says."

"*Flatiron*? Like the hair thing? That makes you go from frizz to fab in the summers?"

"I've trained you well," Libby says. "Something like that. Google says the architect of the Flatiron Building 'hanged himself after it was completed, because he forgot to put in a men's restroom and was humiliated.'"

I guess I'm not peeing there.

"Oh my God!" Libby says, and I can practically feel her smiling. "I'm at Google Maps, and under Nearby Places of Interest there's an entire— Are you sitting for this, Nate?"

"No, I'm literally opposite-of-sitting. I'm looking for a bathroom and avoiding muggers." A cab honks and then another one does, but not at me: just at the air. Everything is so jubilant here.

"There's a *Museum of Sex,* like, *two blocks away from you,*" Libby says, and we howl for about forty minutes over that one. When I come up for air, passing (I'm not kidding) another cupcake place, I say, "A Museum of Sex. Good golly, I wonder what the entry fee is. Like, a kiss?"

Thinking this a pretty good joke, I'm disappointed

and humbled when Libby says, "You're so PG, Nate. I can't wait until you act PG-13. And I'm going to throw a party when you're R."

But I ignore her.

"Okay, Libby: Where am I heading? It's getting really dark and the buildings are getting smaller, so it's probably full of poor people down here, poor people who leave their apartments at midnight and rob children of their new yellow and burgundy coats."

It's nowhere near midnight, actually, but still: the drama of it all.

"Oh, Nate, I wish you had a bike; you'd get to your aunt in, like, less time than the *Chu Chem* overture."

Four people, just like that, whip by me on bikes, exposing swollen calves emerging from rolled-up pants. People are *allowed to bicycle at night* in New York City, folks.

"Oh my God!" I look up. "I'm on Broadway! There's a street called Broadway, and I'm on it!" I'm shouting. "Oh, I wish you were here to take my picture! Aaaaah! I always thought Broadway was just a cluster of the greatest theaters on the planet. It's an actual streeeeeet!"

A woman with a broom lingers outside a convenience store, and I smile at her but she sort of swats me away. Man, there's a lot of liquor stores down here.

"Keep walking down Broadway, boss," Libby says,

and then I hear her yell, "Just a sec, Ma, I'll bring you a glass of water in two shakes of a tail." And back to me, "You're going to get to Union Square, and that's going to be awesome—"

"—because an entire scene in *Ragtime* took place there!"

"Yeah," Libby says. "The one where the belty lady in the bad wig" (we'd watched the show in illegal clips on YouTube) "rouses the crowd."

"Oooh! I love the tenor harmony part on that!"

"Well, yell it out, Natey," Libby says, and I can hear the jealousy in her voice overwhelmed only by her excitement for me. She really is the best friend ever, even if—or especially because—she's willing to blackmail my older brother to save my butt. "Stroll through Union Square, which, according to Google, features organic candy corn vendors, *hint-hint*"—Libby should just skip college, I swear to you—"and then walk down, uh . . . Fourth Avenue. Yeah."

"Wow, that sounds so small and far away. And scary." Luckily, I'm passing a Restoration Hardware, and Mom says rich families on the other side of Jankburg buy couches from there, so I'm probably safe for a few blocks, at least.

"I'm sending you down Fourth because you're going to pass the Public Theater, and that's where *A Chorus Line* played."

"Your step-uncle's all-time favorite show!"

"And that's saying something, because he's gayer than a Christmas flag in August." Her voice is bouncing on itself, and I'm sure she's filling a glass of water in the bathroom for her poor sick mom.

"And then I just stay there? Or I walk by *A Chorus Line* or what?"

"You *know* it's not still playing, Nate," she says, slowly, for the first time losing her patience. I know what this sounds like because it's the *starting* tone that every teacher takes with me, and it only goes downhill from there. "Fourth Avenue'll veer right. Just get to a place called Lafayette. Say it back to me, Nate."

"Laf—Laff . . . aye . . ."

"Are you writing any of this down?"

"No," I say, "you know how I feel about pencils."

"Oy. Okay. Lafayette Street, or Avenue, I can't tell on this map. Say it again, Nate."

"Lafayette."

"And stay on it, and just walk and walk past something called Houston Street, just like Houston, Texas." She says this like I've *been* to Texas; she says this like my Poconos escape with Jesus Christ isn't the most exotic trip I've ever taken. "And you're going to see it, Aw Shucks. Aw Shucks at two-seventy-seven Lafayette."

"Two-seventy Lafayette."

"Two-seventy-*seven*," she says, sighing. "Here, Mommy. Here's your water."

I hear Mrs. Jones say, "Thank you, dear," in a voice so fragile and small, it sounds the way a little bird looks, and I say to Libby, "Can I say hi for just a second?"

And a moment later, Mrs. Jones whispers, "Hello, is this Nate the Great?"

And this small act of humanity in the middle of my big act of craziness: It just gets me. I'm reaching Union Square, a promenade of Halloween vendors and restaurants and a Barnes & Noble the size of a brick cruise ship, all for the gawking. And all of this, all of this adventure and novelty, it would be nothing without somebody to share it with.

You just can't have a scene without a co-star.

"I just want you to know, Mrs. Jones," I say, talking fast in a race to get the words out before my tears come, "that you have the best daughter in the world, and have done one heck of a job"—and then I do cry, because I know this is going to be Mrs. Jones's legacy. That Libby is what she'll have given this world, leaving behind a divorce and a little house in Jankburg, PA. "That Libby is like my sister."

And my phone powers off, just like that. And I'm alone again, staring into this Union Square.

I have a Reese's Piece. The almost-last one.

And I hum the evacuation scene from *Miss Saigon* but then switch gears, turning to the tenor part of that great *Ragtime* number, nobody here even noticing, filling this great square with a boy's lonely voice. It boomerangs back, just slightly, off the blinking lights and stone buildings around me, and I'm just about to feel sorry for myself.

I kiss the rabbit foot instead, and imagine Libby giving me notes on my pitch issues.

And she's with me, again.

And I'm off, again.

It Ain't Texas

"I'm trying to get to Houston," I say.

There's a brief interlude where I walk through Union Square (which is like a big, outdoor mall, but colder) and into the Whole Foods to use the bathroom, and then I use my remaining dollar and penny to buy a piece of individually wrapped "artisanal caramel," and flip through a magazine on modern decor at the register.

Moving ahead.

So I'm on Fourth Street or Road or whatever, now, and looking for this Lafayette Road.

"I'm trying to get to Houston," I say to the most helpful-looking person I see, basically the only person I can find who *isn't* texting somebody.

"Houston, Texas?" she asks. "Because you're very far away from the airports."

"Houston the Avenue, please."

"Houston the . . . ? Oh. Oh, gosh." She squats down so that her face is right in line with my furry hood. "I know it's weird, but in New York we actually pronounce it *How*-ston, not *Hue*-ston."

"Well," I say, "*How* do you do, *How*-ston?"

It's as horrible a joke as it probably reads, really shameful. "*Hue* do you do?" would have been the pun. I always think of the right punch line thirty seconds to three days after the setup; Libby's working on my reflexes.

The lady stands, and her joints crickle-crackle, like Mr. Garret Charles the choreographer's, and this reminds me that I haven't heard anything from *E.T.: The Musical*—also that my phone is dead—and that I've got to get to my aunt's restaurant, lickety-splits.

God, I wish I could do the splits.

"Houston," the lady says, pointing, "is just that way, about five or ten more minutes." Everything is five minutes from the other thing here. It's so cool. "So good luck."

And yet! Another fifteen minutes: my legs getting weak, that dollar-caramel losing its kick, my bookbag growing heavy. I haven't seen a cupcake place in miles and years, by the way, *that's* how long this journey is.

But I've got to get to Aw Shucks.

From a reporter basis, it's important to say that there are a lot of characters down here. That every two blocks the people have gotten incrementally more colorful, hairstyles shifting from basic buzz cuts (Union Square) to Mohawks (Astor Place), now to various shades of pink and lime, practically making me hungry for a popsicle if I weren't so cold.

A man ahead of me is riding an electric scooter (a grown-up is!), and I follow him, mesmerized, and stop just as he's going into a loud, thumping building with shaded-out windows. Another man, twice the size of the scooter guy, guards the door. He's in a T-shirt (a T-shirt in October!) and asking to see the scooter guy's ID. And when the door opens, electric lights paint the walls a garish, thrilling pink. The color of people's hair down here.

I stop on the sidewalk for a sec, my throat aching in the cold.

At first I think there's some kind of emergency inside the thumping building. Everyone's hands are in the air, and the music doesn't sound like music at all, it sounds like a public service announcement played on fast-forward, with sirens and some kind of pumping bass drum underneath it. But a passing ceiling strobe washes over a young guy's face. He's, what, five years older than me? Ten? The guy is surrounded by other people his age, all pulsing against each other, and my initial instinct is to yell, "Somebody help!" In my experience, *that* many people encircling another guy usually ends in a trip to the nurse's office, or worse, to the hospital for stitches.

(This happened once—I was singing "Phantom of the Opera" in the school bathroom, after Libby rented the movie. I thought nobody else was in the stalls, but turns out somebody was taking a two and started audio-recording me on his phone, and he posted it online and I got razzed for months. The kid elbowed my head on his way out of the stall. He didn't wash his hands after, by the way; it is a fundamental fact that bullies don't wash their hands. And my lip split so badly, the nurse sent me to the hospital. I begged to go to the dinky clinic in Jankburg, but they drove me downtown to UPMC. Somewhere in my school file it said my dad was on staff there, but I just didn't want him to see me like this. Didn't want him to see the proof that I couldn't defend myself, not with repeated *Rocky* viewings, not even with a YMCA class on jujitsu, none of it. Four stitches that day, not even a big, impressive number. Not even thirteen stitches, enough that I could have mumbled to my dad: "You shoulda seen the *other* sixth grader.")

But enough about the old me.

Here I am now, holding my bag, standing on the sidewalk just past Houston on Lafayette. The fogged-glass door to the club gets stuck in the wind, and the security guard is deep into a conversation on his cell phone, and I gain this perfect portal into a world I'm not even allowed into, not for so many years. For forever.

A world where guys who look like me and probably liked the *Phantom* movie, too, can dance next to other guys who probably liked *Phantom* and not get threatened or assaulted.

And this one young guy I'm looking at, who's modeling an underbite just like mine, and a little earring? He's smiling such a goofy smile that I'm afraid he's asking for it. That someone's going to snap, and punch him. And just when I gasp, when I see another guy in a denim jacket coming at him, the security guard hangs up and kicks the door closed.

And just before it clicks shut, and I run to it, unaware where I am for a moment, like I'm watching a movie? The two boys kiss.

And nobody punches them.

And the door slams and the building thumps. And thumps. And so does my heart, just one beat ahead of the song inside.

Enter: Oysters

Like a mirage, just when I might sit on the curb and inspect my tired feet to make sure my toes haven't fallen off, I see it: a swinging lit sign, an illustrated oyster in roller skates with a big stupid grin on his face.

Aw Shucks, indeedly-do.

You'd think I'd burst through the door, hunting for an outlet to plug in my phone, begging for a glass of water, falling into Aunt Heidi's arms as her long-lost (recently-lost-again) nephew. But I just stand here, staring through the storefront glass at a long stretch of marble counter. And I don't know what I'm going to say when I get inside.

"Nate?"

Luckily, fate steps in.

"Oh!"

At this evening's performance, the role of Fate will be played by my Aunt Heidi.

I whirl around in my coat, and she's right beside me on the curb, her starched white shirt tucked into black pants. A ponytail makes her look simultaneously younger, like a schoolgirl in a uniform, and older, too, the severity of just a face framed by that swinging hair.

"*What* are you doing here?"

I almost ask her the same thing. A friend of hers (I know because he's in the same outfit as she is, other than the ponytail) is staring at us from against the painted-white walls of the building's exterior.

"I—I missed my bus?" I try. Weak.

"Oh my God, Nate," she says. She looks like she's going to laugh or murder me. I've come to recognize this as the signature look people over the age of thirty give me.

"I—I . . ." But I've got nothing, actually.

She turns around to glance at her friend, dropping her hands to whap them against her thighs. "This is him." She's been talking about me.

"I figured," the guy says, his eyes twinkling. "Though I can't believe you didn't tell me about his amazing, huge jacket," and he strides past us and into the restaurant.

"Oh, yeah," I say, looking down at my coat, "this is new."

"I gathered as much," Heidi says, but she looks

like she's in one of those Japanese terror movies, her mouth not syncing up with the words. She looks, in fact, like I've just burned down her house, or worse—that I actually *am* Godzilla.

"I know I have a lot to explain," I say, "but could I use the restroom inside for a second?"

A moment later, I'm inside a very chic little bathroom with a porthole mirror and swing-arm bronze lanterns, just like we're in a ship. A candle burns in the corner, and I see all sorts of newspaper clippings, *New York Times* write-ups about Aw Shucks. My aunt, of course, is the coolest person in our family and would only work at the kind of restaurant that gets reviewed. Back home, the only restaurants that get written up are those that violate health codes.

When I get out, her friend—the twinkly guy with a face of freckles and cool retro glasses—is standing by the bathroom door. "Your Aunt Heidi asked me to seat you at the far end of the bar," he says, leading me right back to the entrance and pulling out a towering wooden stool for me. "She'll be here in a second."

Am I supposed to tip him?

But he's gone, dashing to the other end of the bar and around the side, grabbing a fizzy drink for somebody.

The whole place is done up like a New England fish shack (I saw *Jaws* at a sleepover once), with shipping maps on the walls and stuffed seagulls in the corner. It's really cool, like a restaurant going as another restaurant for Halloween.

A moment later, Aunt Heidi's freckly friend comes back to me. "Can I get you something to drink? It's on the house."

Whoa! "What was that person having, down there? Thank you, by the way. What's that fizzy thing?"

He smiles. "That's The Heidi. It's named after your aunt. You can't have that, unless you're twenty-one. And just really tiny."

He'd die if I showed him my ID. That would be such a good joke right now, but my bookbag's on the floor and this stool is so high that I'd probably kill myself scaling down the side. "What do you recommend that I'm old enough for?" I say.

"Oh, wow. Mmm. You like Shirley Temples?"

"Only when she's dancing on a staircase," I want to say, but am worried it'll seem sissy to this nice guy, so I just go, "Oh, I gave up Shirley Temples a couple years ago," completely serious, and he laughs for some reason. "Do bars serve hot chocolate?" I'm thinking to ask, when he says: "How about a Sprite, then?"

"Okey-dokey."

He puts it down in front of me and reaches below the bar, producing a beautiful bowl shaped like a shell (they have thought of *everything* here; it's so themey

I practically expect a wave to hit me), filled with Goldfish pretzels.

"How much are these?" I say. I've only a penny left to my name.

"Aw, these are free to any nephew of Heidi's," he says, and turns around to grab somebody a drink.

A guy next to me is flicking through the news on his iPhone and I push back my seat, without thinking, and hop down the thirty or so stories to the floor, yanking out my phone, now on my hands and knees searching for an outlet.

"What are you *doing*?"

I whack my head into a copper foot bar on the stool. "Oh, hi, Aunt Heidi. I'm just looking for a plug."

She doesn't even have to say anything. I just stand.

"You know I *work* here, right?" she says. "That this is really awkward? Can you explain to me in forty seconds or less—because I have a table full of Southern business executives, and I can practically smell their per diem and need to get them their fried clams—why you're still in New York?"

"Well, I—"

"And if your mother knows anything about this yet?"

I jump up to my seat and think about taking a handful of Goldfish pretzels, to stall, but Heidi's really got to get back to those Southern guys.

"I'll be honest, Aunt Heidi—"

"That's a first," she says, arms crossed, a small cocktail-sauce stain where her heart is.

"To be honest," I start again, "I lied. I—I got on the bus and got a message from the casting people, and they wanted me to come back and sing for them. Today."

I take a swig of Sprite.

"Okay?" Heidi says, her eyes doing the Manhattan Dart. She waves to somebody in the back, not a friendly Disney-princess wave but an I'll-be-right-there-when-I'm-through-strangling-my-nephew wave.

"And after the callback, I talked to my friend Libby."

"The underwear explorer," Aunt Heidi says, which is *technically accurate* but a little rude.

"Yep. The underwear explorer. She and I talked, and she's just . . . *covering* for me back home. While I work things out here."

Aunt Heidi cackles, throwing her head back (she'd make a great Witch in *Into the Woods*), eyebrows frantic and mouth twitching. "You are *twelve* years old, Nate. *What* are you 'working out'?"

"I'm nearly fourteen, actually," I want to say, but I actually just go, "Um."

"Heidi," her freckled bartender friend says, "Mitch is kind of ticked off."

Mitch is the manager. I know that in one second flat.

"Stay here," Heidi says, turning from me and then doubling right back, "and I mean it, Nathan."

Freckles the bartender refills my Sprite, without me even asking, and throws a cherry on top, probably because he senses I'm about to lose it and am in need of something sweet. He puts his elbows on the bar top. "You want a salad or something? Do kids eat salads?"

"Some kids do," I say. "Rich kids across town whose schools have salad bars instead of just Jell-O," I'm about to add, but I just say, "Thanks anyway. Not tonight."

"How about some pasta? We've got a shrimp-over-penne thing, topped with a homemade vodka sauce."

"That's nice, sir, but my parents would never let me drink vodka."

I don't know why, but he giggles. "So you're from Pittsburgh, huh, Nathan?"

"Forty-five minutes outside of, but yes." How does he know all this? And do I tell him it's just "Nate," and risk stuttering?

"You might want to tiptoe around your Aunt Heidi, a little," he says. "I know she was already really freaked out that you weren't going to make it back to Pittsburgh alive, and seeing you show up here? I have a feeling it's thrown her for a loop." He shines a glass.

The guy reading the news on his iPhone looks up

at us and reaches across, scooping a few pretzels. "You mind?" he says, and I say, "No problem, sir, they're for everyone."

Freckles turns around, back to where Heidi disappeared, and whispers to me, "You *know*, your Aunt Heidi is quite the actress herself."

"Oh, really?" I say, licking the pretzel bowl clean. He refills my Sprite glass again, with two more cherries this time. Man, I'm downing this stuff like it's—well, a Shirley Temple, which I never actually gave up.

"Yeah," Freckles says, "we did a production of *Midsummer* in Cleveland three years ago. And she was luminous."

Beautiful word if I knew what the heck it meant.

"So why isn't Aunt Heidi still acting?" I say.

"Tough business," Freckles says, stepping back, wiping his hands on a bar towel tucked into his little waist; no adult man where I'm from has a waist so trim. "And she got some weirdly bad notices for *Midsummer*—we met there and became BFFs—and after, she kind of said she was going to take a break. She went to Scottsdale for a couple of weeks and came back wearing a lot of turquoise. And now she just kind of works here all the time."

I'm stuck on the fact that anyone over fifteen is using the term "BFF."

"And are you still an actor?" I say. "I had my first audition ever today."

"Aw, that's great. Yeah, your Aunt Heidi was telling me. I really respect singers a lot."

He does? "You do?"

"Yup, if I could sing, I'd be a total star," and Freckles winks at me. A town of winkers, that's for certain. "But believe me, being another guy with another NYU undergrad degree in acting, it's like there's a zillion of us actors here."

A zillion!

I bet Pittsburgh doesn't even have a *million* actors. I bet Pittsburgh doesn't even have a zillion people of *any* profession.

"And how did your audition go?" Freckles says, chopping a lemon.

"Oh, pretty good, I guess." I just can't believe I'm talking about theater with another guy and he's not slamming my face into a toilet. "There was a British guy who was kind of mean to me—"

"Ugh, they always are," Freckles says. "Really condescending? Talking to you like you're an idiot and wouldn't be able to handle 'the language' because you're American?" Freckles is working himself up a little, the top button of his white shirt straining.

"Yeah. And I said something about Hamlet taking place in 1400, and that kind of irked him."

Freckles says, "Ha ha," like a machine gun, and then, "Well, at least you sing." Talking to me like I'm a real actor. "Try being a classical actor and born in

Utah. Hard to be taken seriously." I'm pretty sure a glass, from behind the bar, breaks in his hand, because he says the S-word and crouches down, and then a "one minute" finger appears from behind the bar, and he's up, his face red. "Wow, I really can't believe I'm, like, vomiting all this to a twelve-year-old."

"I'm almost fourteen," I say. "So don't worry about it."

"Ha," he says, this time like a single bullet. And then, "So what do you like about New York so much? That you would venture all the way here and not tell anyone?"

"Two boys were dancing together in a club," I want to say, "and nobody stopped them." But instead I say, "I want to be on Broadway, and you can't do that forty-five minutes outside of Pittsburgh. Have you ever been to Pittsburgh?"

"Yes, actually. Right out of college, I did a kind of bad postmodern Chekhov thing, set in the Holocaust era—which is just *always* a really bad idea—at the Public Theater."

Ah, yeah, the Pittsburgh Public. I asked Mom if I could see a show there, once, but she said the themes were too adult, switching on another Disney movie in the VCR. We don't even have a DVD player.

Now, I would do anything to sit through Freckles's bad Holocaust production of Chekhov. My new hero Freckles.

"But you're right, Nathan. Even when you live in Astoria, there's nothing like New York."

"I know!" I say. "There's cupcake places, like, everywhere, and boys can dance next to each other." But I don't actually say the part after the cupcake part.

"Cupcake places," Freckles says, twinkling again. I guess he hasn't stopped to think about what's so great in New York, in a while.

"And, you know?" I say. "The Broadway thing? It's just—it's my dream. I know that sounds so cheesy—"

"It doesn't," Mr. Freckles says.

"It's my one chance out of Jankburg."

It feels good to say these words to someone who isn't my guidance counselor, especially because my guidance counselor also doubles as the track coach, and hates me.

"Well, you two are getting along fine," Heidi says, returning with an empty tray. "Okay, so here's the deal, Nate. I'm calling your mom on my next break, and we're sorting this out. I'm really, really unhappy right now, and glad you're alive but really resentful at being put in this position."

"I'm so sorry, Aunt Heidi," I say. I place my phone and charger on the bar and put my head down.

When I look up again, Aunt Heidi is shaking her head at me. "This is just a lot of trouble, Nate, you know that?" She whaps the tray against her hip. "A lot of trouble."

And I guess I must burst into tears again, because here I am seeing my stupid face in the bathroom's porthole mirror, which now just feels idiotic. Like, *what* is this place trying to be? Just admit you're in New York, don't act like you're some kind of boat that serves food, right? Am I right?

I can smell myself in the bathroom and wish I'd brought my bag, to swipe some old non-Mitchum deodorant, wondering if Freckles was on to my changing-body routine. If I've embarrassed myself in front of an actual nice man. And this makes me cry harder. That my one chance at making friends with another boy, even if he's a million years older than me (Freckles is at least twenty-five and maybe even thirty) is ruined, probably. Further soiled by me drinking all his free drinks, like a stupid freeloader, not even tipping him for all the expensive cherries he keeps throwing on top.

I think I'm about to throw up, and run to the toilet (with a wooden seat, like we're in *Maine*), but I just end up with the hiccups, rendering me even more fragile and stupid and unable to control myself.

And when I finally get back to the bar, hiccupping and burping and reconvinced that Freckles hates me, he's standing there with Heidi, and they're both kind of frowning. And now she's holding her tray like it's a teddy bear.

"We plugged your phone in," Freckles says, handling it like evidence, a murder weapon.

"Okay," I say, or hiccup.

"And you got a call while you were in the bathroom," Heidi says, her face in a bunch of angles, like a Picasso.

"Okay," Hiccup. Pause. Hiccup-hiccup.

"And I just picked up," Heidi says, overexplaining, "not looking, thinking maybe it was your mom."

"She even said, 'Sherrie, is this you?' and everything," Freckles says. He puts my phone down and refills my Sprite.

"But it wasn't your mom," Heidi says, and she pats the stool seat and I jump up. "It was the *E.T.* casting people."

"They called?" I say, or yell, and of course I hiccup and leap to my feet and knock the fresh Sprite to its side. All over Freckles.

And that's when I know it's bad news. Because he doesn't even look mad at me.

"They said you're a little too old to play Elliott," Heidi says. "They don't need to see you again, Nate. You can just . . . you're free to go home now. It's . . . it's over."

I don't believe it. "I don't believe you. I—"

But she holds up my phone: a seventeen-second phone call logged from an incoming 212 number. Broadway's area code.

"They don't want to see me again? At all?"

"I'm sorry."

Seventeen seconds was all it took.

And then, just like that, my hiccups are gone.

The Next Part

I go to the bathroom again (for the third time! Freckles probably thinks I have a bowel condition or something).

And cry so hard that a foam of spit blasts out across the framed reviews for Aw Shucks.

It's just pretty embarrassing and I don't need to go into it here, okay?

You'd think, the way I'm crying, that I'd *died*. And not that just my dreams and soul had.

After I leave the bathroom, having pulled my bangs as far over my eyes as possible, Freckles tells me he didn't get *his* first job until after his tenth audition in New York. "So every no is closer to a yes, huh, buddy?"

But it's not working.

It's back to Jankburg. And rifles and bad test grades and grey fields full of grey cows, and—oh, God. The bathroom. To cry it out just one last time I swear.

A Couch That Thinks It's an Envelope

"It's really cool," I say, surveying Aunt Heidi's futon. "I've never seen anything like this." I open and close it, folding it back and forth on itself. "A couch that thinks it's an envelope or something," I say, and Freckles and Heidi laugh. Turns out they're roommates.

"You must be exhausted," Aunt Heidi says. Because she is, I'm sure.

"I'm actually completely wound up," I say. And I am.

"Let me run you a bath."

I don't have the heart to tell her that I haven't taken a bath for a hundred years. Freckles and I sit on the futon, and he kicks his shoes off. He's in funny socks.

"You're looking at my funny socks, huh?"

"Nah," I say.

"Dressy socks," he says, wiggling his toes. "Church socks, every Sunday."

Huh. Freckles goes to church?

"Big day, huh?" he says.

I remove my giant coat and then, remembering that I stink, place it over myself like a blanket.

"You cold?" Freckles says. "Because we've got blankets.

"Oh no, no, I'm fine, thanks." Their place is smaller than I could have even imagined. All those *Friends* reruns, the soaring loft ceilings and funky-colored walls? Nope. It's a bare white box and big clanking pipes and one framed show poster from a production of *Grand Hotel* at Walnut Street Theater.

It's heaven, though.

Freckles turns the TV on, pretuned to a channel that broadcasts only New York news, which is amazing.

"I wonder if I could get this back home," I say. "Oh God, home. I should call Libby."

"You want me to leave you alone?" Freckles asks.

"Well, I don't want to annoy you." Dad hates when I talk on my cell phone during Steelers games, even if I'm in my own bedroom.

"Nah, but why don't you go into Heidi's room, for privacy?"

A moment later I'm sitting on Aunt Heidi's floor, not wanting to disturb the bed. A kitty circles me.

"Libby?"

"Oh, boy, how are *you*?" she says.

"I'm okay. I'm at my Aunt Heidi's. It's been a rough night."

"You're telling me. They called off the neighborhood search when your aunt got through to your mom."

I wish I could just pause time or fast-forward or something. I don't even want to hear, but still: "What—what did my mom say?"

"She was going to call my mom and rat me out for lying about Extreme Hide-and-Seek, but I did the crying thing again and everyone oohed and aahed and just told me to get lost," Libby says. "So I'm home now, waiting for you to call."

"Is your mom okay?"

"She's asleep."

"Is Anthony okay?" I can't believe I'm asking about *him*.

"Yeah, sure. I mean, he won't be playing for six weeks or something, which is sort of devastating to him."

"Right."

"So did you hear anything else about *E.T.*?"

"Yeah." I swallow and look at the cat. "I didn't get farther. They—I guess they just weren't looking for little boys my age."

"Oh, that's weird," Libby says, "because Jordan

Rylance posted something on Insta that he has a callback for Elliott tomorrow, and the whole world Liked it. As if he already got the part or whatever."

She just shouldn't have said that, and we both know it, immediately, and I basically want to melt into the floor and let Aunt Heidi's kitty eat me as dinner.

"Wow, good for Jordan Rylance," I say, just as sarcastically as you can imagine a guy like me'd say it.

"You're back home tomorrow, though?" Libby says. She doesn't usually let me see her this hopeful and vulnerable, so it's kind of nice.

"Yeah, we're waking up at, like, five a.m. and going back to the bus station, and I'll be home in time for the last class of the day, I'm sure. I'm sure Mom'll make me go right to school, and then I'll get home with twelve hours of homework and they'll ground me and not even let me Trick-or-Treat." Aunt Heidi's cat, I see as my eyes adjust, is jet black. And crossing me. "Or Dad'll just kill me, actually. And then send my body to school the next day."

"Well," Libby says, "at least I'll be there. And luckily, you already sort of act like a corpse in class."

"Yeah," I say. And then I brighten for her. "Yeah, it'll be great to see you. This whole thing has been . . . really overwhelming."

"You'll have to tell me every single moment, or act it out, when we're face to face in my basement."

But I know I won't be able to. That to talk about New York would mean to remember everything I'm leaving, everything I didn't get to get used to. Just to get a taste of. Even the Chevys chips were better than the ones back home, and I'd know, because I had two baskets.

I hang up. Heidi's still in the bathroom, the water running on full blast, and Freckles is sitting on the futon with his laptop out. "Everything cool?" he says.

"Yeah, that was just my best friend."

"The underwear kid?" I expect him to say, but he just goes, "It's good to have a best friend," like I'm seven years old or something and up next he's going to teach me the difference between circles and squares.

I sit criss-cross on the futon and can feel the weight of the day on my head, my eyes drift.

Heidi comes out of the bathroom, having done a total costume change, standing there in sweats and an old Pitt T-shirt, looking like college photos Mom used to have of her. Before she put them all away.

"Okay, Natey, the bathroom's all yours," she says.

I hop in the bath and, come to think of, maybe I should take them more often. It's like a big wet hug, in a good way. And something about seeing my body reflected back at me, like I'm looking at somebody else's? It's just not as bad as I might have thought.

I close my eyes and wince, thinking about the

return to Jankburg, and I sink to the bottom, below the layer of bubbles Aunt Heidi put in. And for a second, underwater, I nod off, asleep or maybe even hoping to drown.

If I have to die—and according to everyone I go to school with, I have to die often, and soon—it might as well be in New York.

It's Like a Bed but Stranger and Lumpier and with More Wooden Slats, and Hidden Crumbs

If you've never been tucked into a futon, you don't know what you're missing.

"Night, Nate."

You're missing nothing, I meant.

"Night, Aunt Heidi."

She flips the lamp off, next to the couch/futon/bed thing, and asks me if I've got enough blankets, and then, just when a normal person would go back to her own bed, she stays.

"Should I keep the kitchen light on?" she asks, shaking an old travel clock, distracting herself with an object like adults always do. "You going to be okay overnight?" She probably knows I've never really slept anywhere other than my room and Libby's floor.

"Oh, sure," I say, "thirteen-year-olds can sleep anywhere."

"Ah, well, that's good."

She's looking at me like I'm dying or she'll never see me again. Both of which might be likely. It's one thing to be old, to be forty or fifty with a broken heart, but it's practically terminal when you're thirteen. When you're thirteen with a broken heart, I bet your valves aren't even strong enough to mend themselves.

"I'm really sorry for causing you all this trouble," I say, sitting up so I don't fall asleep. "I hope Mitch didn't fire you or anything."

She makes a face. "How did you know my boss's name was Mitch?"

"I overheard Freckles talking to you about it."

"You're very observant," she says. "But, no, I'm not fired. It's all good."

"I found pictures of you when you were in the bathroom," I say.

"What do you mean?" she asks.

"There was a binder of old show photos, underneath the futon." She rolls her eyes. "No, they're great," I say. "They really are. Freckles and I were making the futon up, and then I found them and started looking. You were really beautiful."

She grunts. You're not supposed to say stuff like that to girls.

"No, I mean, you still are. You just had so much makeup on in those photos. It was really something."

"Yes, well—any help I could get," she says, and

a siren roars outside. I must have flipped my head around, really fast, because she says, "Don't worry, happens all the time."

"My friend's step-uncle lives in Queens, too," I say for some reason. "So it's cool that you live out here. Seems like an amazing coincidence." My head is getting heavy.

"Not such a coincidence," she says, and now she picks up the binder of old show pictures. She's tracing her initials, I can tell, into the leather cover. Distracting herself. "Everyone who almost-made-it-but-didn't lives in Queens," and she laughs to cover how pitiful she knows that sounded.

I gather the blankets around my waist and conceal a yawn, hugging a scratchy throw pillow, and then start into her. "Why do you say 'almost made it'? You were luminous in Cleveland, according to Freckles."

She laughs again.

"He told me at your restaurant. It's an amazing restaurant, by the way."

"Yeah," she says, "the specials are really good on the weekends. And—" She catches herself, about to tell me there's a drink named after her. About to repeat her routine.

"So why did you stop acting, for real?"

"Oh, Nate," she says, and stands, putting the binder of photos underneath the coffee table, and then placing two hardcover books on top of it, and a remote control, and when that isn't "hidden" enough, a paperweight on top of it too. "It's just—this kind of lifestyle isn't for everybody, you know? It's tough and there's a lot of rejection, and . . ." She looks at me hard. "You know that little hurt you felt today—or big hurt—when *E.T.* released you? It's tough getting used to it." My stomach drops; I'd almost forgotten about it. "I'm not sure you ever do."

"Do you love working at Aw Shucks?"

"Do I *love* working at Aw Shucks? No, Nate, no I don't. But I—you know, the tips are good and I believe in the product, and your friend Freckles keeps me company. It's not a bad gig. While I figure things out." Her voice catches.

"Do you have a boyfriend?"

"Oy. Nate. The interrogation."

I'm silent, which probably seems like a tactic, but actually I just don't know what to say.

"I dated this guy, Troy, for a long time. I've *been* dating this guy, Troy, for a long time."

"Well, that's cool," I say.

"Yeah," she says, looking at something on the table next to me. Maybe the cat leapt up, or a cockroach is about to attack me. That happens a lot here, Libby says. "Yeah, it's cool. It would just be nice to know where it's going."

"You mean you're not getting married?"

"Not yet, at least," she says, tilting her head at me. "Yeah, he's not sure about marriage. This is after seven years together, off and on."

Seven!, I think. "You're like Adelaide in *Guys and Dolls*, but your voice isn't annoying," I almost say.

"And there was a blonde-and-mysteriously-younger girl that a friend of mine saw Troy out with a few months ago, and he still hasn't come up with a particularly satisfactory answer for that. So. Yeah."

I scrunch my nose and blink a couple times.

"Well," she says, "I've always got those old show photos," kind of kicking the coffee table, and she takes her hair out of a rubber band and repositions it. Girls are so lucky because they have so many props. "I'm just going to be quiet now," Heidi says, and stands, but even then she doesn't really move.

"I wish I lived here," I say. "I wish I could see you every day. I think we'd have a lot of fun and probably teach each other valuable lessons and somebody would write a movie about it. And we'd play ourselves." She smiles and then snorts a little and that, finally, makes me smile, my underbite cramping. I guess I haven't smiled in ages. "Yeah. I wish I lived right next door to you, or even on this futon."

She grabs my big toe at the end of the bed, shaking it under the blanket. "I do too, Natey. You're really sweet. It's nice—it's nice to see that you're growing up so sweet."

And suddenly she's definitely crying.

"What's wrong, Aunt Heidi?" I say.

She shakes her head and gulps. "It's just like I'm seeing myself in you, is all. It's just that I'm trying to remember what it felt like when even Times Square seemed cool, and not like just another mall."

I actually love malls, but I think I know what she means. But boy, are malls fun.

"So what? Do you just work at Aw Shucks forever?"

"Gosh," she says, squeezing my toe, "you sound like my shrink."

So it's true. People *do* stay up all night here—it's after midnight and I can hear Freckles doing push-ups in his room, listening to vintage Madonna—*and* everyone has a shrink here. It's no big thing, though. It's just New York. It's just what it's like to be a New Yorker, it's not that deep.

"I don't know. I either work at Aw Shucks forever or Troy asks me to marry him and I have babies," she says, laughing at herself. "Like, in the next twelve minutes"—she points to a wristwatch that isn't even there—"I have a baby. Or I don't. Ever."

Freckles turns Madonna up a little louder, probably overhearing us. Probably sick of hearing Aunt Heidi talking about babies, which I bet you she does a lot.

"Okay, I'm going to bed. I'm going to bed, Nate," and she turns off the kitchen light, reachable from the futon, and kisses me on the forehead.

"You'll wake me up in the morning, before the bus?"

"Sure thing, Nate."

"And Aunt Heidi?"

"Yes?"

"I think you should make up with Mom."

She stops tucking and just sort of shifts her jaw at me, frozen. "Good night, Nate."

Coat of Many Colors

I know you're not supposed to write about your dreams.

Libby told me that it is a scientific fact that *nobody*, other than Joseph in *Joseph and the Amazing Technicolor Dreamcoat* (hilarious songs in that one, by the way), is interested in your dreams.

Though I bet Aunt Heidi's shrink listens to Aunt Heidi's dreams all the time, and I'm ninety percent sure they always involve babies, or Troy.

Anyway, overnight on the futon I had a pretty cool dream, but you can skip this paragraph and just go to the *section below, if you don't care.

An amazing thing happened in this dream. I was in the bathroom back at Aw Shucks (all my dreams are literal; I would die to slay a dragon or be able to fly, just one night) and I got out and Aunt Heidi and Freckles were standing there, just like they were in real life. He was holding my cell phone and she had my bookbag, except instead of frowns, they wore grins.

"The casting office called," Aunt Heidi said, in the dream. And I did the same thing as in life, except for spilling the Sprite on Freckles. In the dream, Freckles lifted me up and put me on his strong shoulders, and in the dream the Aw Shucks ceiling was another three feet high, so I didn't hit my head. And Aunt Heidi stood atop my stool (you know it was a dream because girls after the age of eighteen always hate doing stuff like that, climbing stuff, and especially moms hate putting their heads under water at the Y pool after they've been to the beauty shop), and Aunt Heidi yelled out: "Listen up, everyone! My nephew Nate Foster is Elliott in *E.T.: The Musical*!"

And John Williams, who wrote the awesome movie score, happened to be at the bar, slurping on an oyster, and he leaned over to me and said, "You're not missing anything; these oysters taste like a flipper."

Then John Williams began conducting the amazing flying sequence, of E.T. going across the moon on the bike. I'm not sure where all the instrument sounds came from at the bar, but still. It's a dream.

The clearest part is that Freckles lowered me to the floor, behind the bar, and gave me The Heidi—the fizzy adult drink I wasn't allowed to try—just because finally being on Broadway: Basically I was an adult anyway. And he started shaking my shoulders and saying, "You know what this means? It means you don't have to face those boys back at school. It means you don't have to go back to classes that you daydream through. It means you never have to throw another basketball in another mandatory P.E. class. It means you don't have to suffer through your dad asking you if you've met any cute girls yet."

And I took a big fizzy slurp of The Heidi, and hiccupped, just like in life but less related to how upset my stomach was, and Aunt Heidi flipped me around and shook my shoulders too, shouting, "I'm so proud of you, Nate!"

And that takes us to the present.

"Nate! Nate!" I can't remember the last time I woke up with a smile, Aunt Heidi's long hair sweeping my forehead, my body wrapped in a hundred old blankets, swirled around me like soft-serve. I must have really tossed and turned, and (for the record) the one thing Western Pennsylvania has over New York is a better bed situation. Yikes, futons *suck*.

"Nate!" She's shaking my shoulders, just like in my dream, except instead of John Williams's score playing, there's sirens in the background, again, and the tick of a coffee machine.

"Eh?" I sit up, practically head-butting Aunt Heidi.

"Get up, right away," she says, and I blink a bunch and say, "Is it time already?"

"I'll explain in a second." She's listening to somebody shouting through her cell phone, and jogs away from me back into her bedroom.

I swing my legs around (futons *are* really low to the ground, so that's one asset for a midget like me) and stand up, my knees cracking. A rite of passage! It's like New York has grown my joints up, if not my feelings.

Heidi calls out, "Hop in the bath, quick," and hurries me in. I pass the kitchen and see 3:44 on the microwave, and that just seems weird. Gosh, we're up early.

Ten minutes later, when I'm through with the scrubbing routine (she and Freckles share a lot of really cool bath products, including a whole Kiehl's thing that's made out of kale and lye, according to the packaging), I towel off and look in the mirror. And if I'm not mistaken, I catch sight of a teeny tiny moustache. I don't want to get all worked up about it—there's the chance I forgot to wash my face and this might just be a rim of chocolate from the hot cocoa Aunt Heidi made me before bedtime last night—but it's nice to see what I might look like in a few years.

Oh, wait, a zit. Great.

Knock knock from outside. "Hurry up, Nate, I

need you to get dressed." Yikes, girls are pushy before sunrise.

I slip on a fresh pair of undies and dig around in their medicine cabinet (there's basically nothing more fun than a harmless peek at someone else's toiletries, right gang?) and Freckles has some cool, exotic Arm & Hammer deodorant that I decide to try. If it works for someone as friendly as him, I might as well give it a test run.

Just as I'm barely exiting the bathroom, Aunt Heidi hands me a glass of orange juice and tells me to sit on the futon. "And stay there. And be ready to go." That part she's really clear about. "Pack up your phone and everything."

I grab my lucky rabbit foot and hold tight. Heidi looks like she's about ready to explode.

The sky is still Pepsi-black, and I wonder if Libby's asleep right now, if she pulled an all-nighter decorating the porch for Halloween tonight. Her house is famous for its dramatic displays, but I'd bet they're scaling back this year, with Mrs. Jones so sick.

I bet when I get home and Dad chops my head off with an axe, I could go as my dead self for Halloween if he throws my face on ice quickly enough. At least I'll get a little candy before they bury me.

But nobody better hand out any Reese's Pieces.

And then, sitting here on the futon, I hear Aunt

Heidi's cell phone ring again from her bedroom, and she runs to an intercom thing by the front door (very cool, very space-age) and presses a buzzing button. She steps out into their hallway, leaving the door an inch ajar.

The heck?

What follows is a growing mumble, two voices starting polite, quiet, like when a lady buys stamps at the post office and gives the minimum amount of respect required to the teller. And as I'm fondling the rabbit foot and making sure my fly is zipped up and wondering if we woke Freckles, out he comes from the bedroom, wearing pajama bottoms and—oh, how funny—no shirt.

"What's up?" he says, rubbing his eyes. Gosh, nobody back home is built like him, other than the varsity swim team. But he's so much older than them, like some animated character: AdultBoyMan, with a high schooler's fatless body and a kind adult's face.

"I dunno," I say, "I think Aunt Heidi's having a fight with someone in the hallway."

He kind of cocks his head back, processing the whole thing, his hair a mess, and yawns. "Why are you dressed?"

"I think to go to the bus station."

"At four a.m.?" he says. He knows something's up, like when Feather could tell we were going to have that one, famous Pittsburgh tornado, and kept knocking Mom's *Sleepless in Seattle* commemorative plates off the wall with his tail. I still swear it wasn't an accident, it was like Feather's warning.

Now Freckles goes and peers through the crack in the door, and steps back, and looks at me, and then peers through again. "Oh, God," he says, and then he jumps out of the way and the door flies open, unhinged.

And there she is.

"Nathan Evan Foster, wait outside."

And Mom—*Mom!*—walks right up to me, stumbling over herself, simultaneously surveying Aunt Heidi's tiny apartment. It's an apartment I've already grown defensive of, loving the fact that, in only five hundred square feet (Freckles and I talked dimensions), there's no chance a burglar is hiding in the attic, waiting to kill you.

Mom grabs me by my wrist, the rabbit foot flying away from me like some crazed infant squirrel, and she flings me across the room, the coffee table dancing behind us. She's a wreck. And it's almost completely my fault.

Also, she called me by my middle name, which I hate for you to hear.

"Get downstairs," she says, "and wait in the Grand Caravan. I'm—I'm serious." Except imagine all of that more slurred. "How could you do this to us, Nathan?"

"I did it for *me*, Mom. Not *to* you."

"We were terrified."

"You don't—you can't know how bad it is in Jankburg. For someone like me. You don't know the words they call me. It gets worse every da—"

"*I've* got some words for you. In the car. *Now.*"

I can feel Freckles holding his own breath.

"I hate you," I say, rushing past Mom to the hallway. And when I think she's going to call out after me, to remind me that "I'd have killed you if you'd gotten yourself killed," she doesn't. She says—so quiet I can barely make it out—"I'd have died if you'd gotten hurt."

Aunt Heidi's still outside the door, her face the color of a robin's chest. Not red, like you might think, but bright amber like a Technicolor fire.

And as I zombie-walk to the elevator, she just touches my shoulder.

"You're not going anywhere with her."

Lobbies Are Just Lobbies: A Weak Metaphor

A minute later I'm in the lobby, and it's really nothing special. It's really just a basic plain lobby, and lemme tell you: If you think everything in New York is high class, like the inside of a yacht or something, it isn't. Sometimes it's just another hallway; sometimes it looks just like your junior high school.

Aunt Heidi's lobby looks like the guidance counselor waiting area back home, a bulletin board here advertising exterminators instead of basketball tryouts; a garbage can overflowing with the *New York Times* instead of the *General Thomas Junior High Gazette*.

(Anthony used to write a sports column for the *Gazette*, when he went to my junior high, but as soon as he left for high school, they lost advertisers. Like, for real.)

Well, the whole thing upstairs is clear.

Just as soon as Mom heard from Heidi, she must have packed up a dusty bottle of booze, jumped in the minivan, and time-warped to New York. She's a heck of a driver, Mom is, when motivated.

I guess her A train wasn't running local this morning.

Mom didn't actually drink and *drive*, by the way. She's not *that* dumb. In the old days, whenever she had to confront something scary, she'd just get to wherever she was going and sit in the car and drink until she got up the courage to go inside. According to her diary.

I walk over to a dying potted plant, in this city full of potted plants, wedged in a corner of Heidi's first floor lobby. Looking like nobody's given it any attention or love in forever. If E.T. were real, we could gauge his health based upon this plant. This plant that he'd bring back to life, just 'cause that's what E.T.s do, that's what they're good at.

When Libby and I stayed up the other night and studied the movie for my audition (*her* mom has a Blu-ray player), I'd forgotten that in the beginning of the movie there's actually a *lot* of E.T.s, like a million, spread out all over that magical forest. And the funniest thing is, all they were doing was looking for plants. They just go to other planets to check out the scene and pick up a few ferns. I wish E.T. were here now and could make this sad plant sprout back up, pop out its planty chest, and make something of itself. I wish everything were healthy. I wish Mom could have just stayed home, back on Planet Jankburg. Could have let me ride out my trip in dignity. Daring myself to come back to New York when I'm old enough. I wish Mom hadn't had something to drink.

My phone rings: 412. Oh, gosh.

"Hello?"

"Nathan Foster."

"Hi. Hi, Dad."

"Is your mother okay? Is she—is she there in one piece?"

"She's okay, Dad. She's here. I—" But I stop. He's heaving for air.

"What in the Lord's name were you thinking, Nathan? Going all the way, without our permission, to a place like New York *City*?"

"I know, Dad. I'm a rotten kid." My throat closes like a fist. "I'm a rotten son. I—I'm grounded until Christmas break, at least. I know you're always praying for me and I . . . I wish it were paying off for you. I really do." I really do. "I was stupid. I'm the stupidest son you have, and it was the stupidest thing I've—"

"Nathan." He swallows. Coughs. Grips the phone so hard, the plastic handset creaks. "It was some kind of brave, boy." *Click*.

Brave?

"Hey, Nate," from behind. I turn around and—oh, God—I guess I'm sobbing a teeny bit, or about to.

Freckles is in jeans now, and a T-shirt and a corduroy jacket and backward ball cap. "Come on, buddy, let's get out of here for a little bit and get you some breakfast. There's a good diner around the corner." And just like that I follow him out onto the drizzly street.

I do that kid thing where I don't say anything. I feel like anything I say will reveal how young I am or how much I don't understand about adults, about my own confusing parents.

"Do you like waffles?" Freckles says, and I want to say, "Is Christine Daaé's high note pre-recorded in *Phantom*?", but it seems too early in the day for that kind of insider stuff (and only Libby'd laugh, because it's her line anyway). So I just go, "Uh-huh."

We order waffles. Well, I do. Freckles orders an egg white omelet (*what?*) and coffee and water, and about a thousand minutes go by before he says, "Well, that was awkward back there, huh?"

"Yes!" I say, and luckily the waiter comes over and sets down toast, for the table, because I can just stuff my mouth and not talk.

"This isn't my business," Freckles says. People always say that just before they try to get you to say secrets and stuff. "But has your mom shown up . . . like that to places before?"

"Oh, a long time ago." I'm mumbling through a mouthful of horrible rye toast, toast that tastes like it was baked three years ago and set out in the sun. "It's an old problem that she sort of has under control." Or had.

The waffles appear out of nowhere—there must be some diner conveyor belt back there—and the waiter sets down a whole jar of syrup for me, in a real glass bottle that's totally sticky and gross but, again, solely for me, which is cool. "Wow, this place is fast," I say like an idiot.

Freckles yawns and drinks his coffee down in about a single gulp, and he giggles and points to lipstick on the rim, and we smile over that one.

"That isn't from me, believe me, Nate. I haven't worn lipstick since college." He laughs at his own joke. "This place isn't known for cleaning their germy dishes, but it'll build up your immunities before you get home. You can go back to Jankburg the strongest little boy around."

"Ha," I say. I like that, that single "ha." I think I picked it up from Freckles and it's fun to employ it so quickly.

Freckles gets a text and looks at this phone, and he says, "Just a sec," and presses a button and steps away from the table and stands in the rain, the drizzle turning into a downpour. A woman walks by the window, and she's wearing a catsuit, a whole catsuit with ears and everything. And that's what's so cool about New York, how much it can open your mind; I barely even did a double take, thinking catsuits were a total norm here, until remembering it's Halloween, that she's actually in costume. That said, I'm pretty sure I saw another lady in a catsuit, yesterday, and it wasn't even Halloween then.

"Okay," Freckles says, sliding back into the booth, "not to rush you or anything, but when you're done, we're going to go back home." Home. I wish. Home on the futon. "Back to my place. Your mom is taking a nap, and Heidi wants to talk to you."

Great. I think about ordering another round of waffles, just to eat up some time, and then remember that it wouldn't be too effective—*that's* how fast the food comes here. I bet they literally have a tree in the back that just grows waffles all day long. A potted city tree, of course.

I'll buy time another way: Ask anyone over twenty-nine about their love life and you can stop the clock cold for fifteen minutes, minimum. (A famous and rare Libby theory.)

"Hey, Freckles," I say—but I call him his real name, which I still haven't told you because I don't like it, so you can just stop wondering—"were you and Aunt Heidi ever boyfriend-girlfriend?"

He laughs and says, "No. Nope, Nate."

"Oh, that's cool."

"Yep." He's scrolling through an e-mail on his iPhone, pretending to listen to me. Adults can never just talk to me without the distraction of some activity keeping them firmly in their own world. Unless I'm being reprimanded at school for forging sick notes from Mom. In that case, adults seem to have no problem at all shutting their phones off and describing what a miserable future a kid like me is setting himself up for.

"She's really pretty, though," I say to Freckles. "Don't you think Heidi's pretty? I think she's really pretty."

"She is, for sure."

"Does she ever talk about a boyfriend?"

Freckles shifts on the banquette and sets his phone aside. "There's some character who's been bouncing around for a while, yeah. I'm sure Heidi can tell you all about Troy. Troy is—very special."

"Like super nice?"

"Oh, like super elusive. Beefy and hunky but . . . I shouldn't . . . it's not really my place to talk about him."

I clear my throat. "Maybe *you* could just date Aunt Heidi, then? And cut out the middleman?"

Freckles licks his lips. "Heidi's not . . . really my type."

"She's so cool, though!" I say.

"She is cool, but I—I date other . . . *men*, Nate."

Oh my gosh. "Oh, wow. Okay, that's cool." I don't want him to feel uncomfortable or judged or anything, so I play it really cool. It's nice that he'd trust such a huge secret to me, though.

"So, yeah," Freckles says, and laughs.

He pays for the waffles and that weird white omelet, and I grab a couple handfuls of (free!) mints by the door (like *completely* free, and already unwrapped, too).

"It's all going to be okay, you know?" Freckles says, leading me back "home," past dumpsters and a pizza place and a few business guys. I like it out here, this Queens scene. It's like a slower, 1950s version of the real city across that cool bridge we cabbed over last night.

"Pittsburgh's got a bunch of bridges too," I say for some stupid reason.

"I remember," Freckles says, "from that Chekhov play I did after NYU. We took publicity shots on a bridge."

"Weird," I say, stepping over an abandoned shoe, "because I didn't think there were any giant bridges with sports stadiums in the background during the

Holocaust." There's a lot of stadiums in Pittsburgh—like one stadium per every normal boy.

Freckles laughs about my Holocaust one-liner, and it doesn't even sound like a condescending adult laugh. It's, like, totally real.

Libby'd be so proud.

We get back to the lobby of his building and walk to the elevator, and I don't want to face her. I don't want to see Mom, who is everything difficult and set at a slower speed, everything forty-five minutes outside of Pittsburgh.

But I swear that, following Freckles from behind, looking at his body in those jeans (they're really, really nice jeans and they fit him really, really well), when we pass that little potted plant in the corner, there's something different about it.

One of the leaves that was falling over—yellowed, dying, drooping like a waterslide that nobody's allowed on—has pumped up a little, is climbing to the window.

Might even be alive.

Split Screen

"Nate, we're so happy you stayed in town," Rex Rollins the casting director says.

(There's a part I skipped over where Mom sobered up.)

"To be honest, Mr. Rollins, I never planned on leaving," I say, my legs not even shaking, rooted again on the centered *x*.

(There's something where Freckles and I got home from the waffle place, and Mom was asleep on the same futon I slept on, and she murmured something about being happy that it smelled like "My Natey.")

"Would you mind just waiting in the hall for ten minutes?" Mark or Marc says. "We're running just a little behind."

(Which might have been the nicest thing my mom has ever said about me. That she likes how I smelled. That she was overjoyed to see me again. That I wasn't punished after all. That she probably just wants her ATM card back.)

"No *problemo*," I say, "I've got no other plans."

(There's a part where Aunt Heidi and Freckles took me out, again, just as soon as we returned from waffles—not back to the diner, but for a walk around the block, to talk about Mom. The rain went away, and every other person was in a Halloween costume. All this, before the sun was barely up. Like New York is so ready for a party, full-on grown-ups are willing to go as Groucho Marx to work, to ride the subway in a scratchy fake moustache.)

"Jordan! I heard from my friend that you got a callback, too. It's, like, the big news on Instagram."

(I didn't know who Groucho Marx was, but Aunt Heidi explained.)

"Oh," Jordan says. "Hi, Nate."

(There's a part, on that walk past grown-up Groucho Marxes and little girls heading off to school in princess dresses, where Aunt Heidi told me I was going to stay in New York another night, because Mom wasn't feeling too hot. Because Dad is with Anthony and the dogs, and might even take them on a guy camping trip. Even with Anthony's calf muscle being torn.)

"Nate, could you just stand against the wall while we measure your height?" the blonde ringlet-haired casting woman says—with no boiling Starbucks in sight.

(There's this part where Aunt Heidi said Mom and Dad had a big fight on their anniversary trip to the Greenbrier in West Virginia. And Mom's distraught, and for the first time in a long time is actually asking *Heidi* for advice. But I didn't want to get into all that here.)

"Absolutely I will," I say, wondering why I need to be measured. "Would you like me in my shoes or out, when I stand against the wall?"

(Because after we'd finally circled their Queens neighborhood so many times that if we were the sun and Heidi's apartment were earth, an entire month would have gone by, my phone rang.)

"Looks good. You're four eight. He's four eight, Rex."

(And *E.T.* called. *E.T.* phoned me. Phoned home.)

"Come on in, Nate," Rex Rollins says. "The team is ready for you again."

(And the director "wasn't satisfied with any of the female little people they'd seen audition for the role of E.T.," the casting director explained to Heidi—when I almost threw up on the sidewalk and she rescued the phone from my quaking hand.)

"Nice to see you all again!" I say, or scream-cry. "I'm sorry I'm auditioning in the same outfit."

(But that they *were* "haunted" by *my* "explosive, nervous, stuttery energy.")

"Would you like me to stand on the *x* again?"

(And while I'm not technically a little person or a puppet expert or a girl, Mr. Garret Charles, of all people, responded to my knee crawls, and could picture me "bringing to life an alien creature with a weird voice and an underbite and a waddle." All the qualities back home that get me nearly killed could actually get me nearly famous, here.)

"That sounds great, Nate, and don't worry about the outfit," says Calvin, the nice assistant director with Ken-doll blond hair.

(And I'd be "reading for the Elliott understudy, too," especially since I have experience covering big roles in the past. Who knew the vegetable pageant would be such a stepping-stone? And could I please come back in today, right away? And could I please be prepared to perform my same monologue for the team? And meet the official director this time?)

(And I sat on a fire hydrant and had a mild hyperventilation. And Freckles and Heidi laughed and laughed and hopped and hopped, looking like two nice people going as two nice parents for Halloween. Parents of one good kid who gets a lot of things wrong, most of the time, back home, but might be getting everything right, here. A kid who might have found someplace where he doesn't have to change anything about himself, to fit in.)

(A kid going as himself for Halloween, but the best version, the ultimate.)

A better Nate than ever.

After the Audition

"Libby-dibby?"

"Natey-the-greaty, what blows?" She's trying out new catchphrases again. I kind of like this one.

"I got a miracle callback this morning! I got a call-back and I'm here, now. I just left the room and they told me to wait in the hallway, so my aunt is buying me a Vitamin Water to celebrate!"

From Libby's end of the call, I can hear familiar locker slams (my heart speed racing in auto-response), and Libby says, "I've only got a sec before last period's over, but I'm so proud of you. Like, beyond. I'm in the science lab hallway, and several people, in fact, are asking me why I'm jumping up and down, and *I'm not telling them.*" She's yelling by the end.

Jordan Rylance comes out of the audition room and sits down next to his leopard-coated mother, who is eyeing me, appropriately, like I'm a gazelle who she's going to drag into a tree and chew the head off of.

"It's been nutso, that's for sure. My mom showed up in a bad state to my aunt's this morning—not kidding." For some reason I say this loudly enough for Mrs. Rylance to hear. Like it's a badge of honor.

"What happened in the *audition*?" Libby always knows how to skip through the murk of a story.

"I met the director, and they made me do my monologue, and—get this—I did the bus speech from the Greyhound Station. And they *loved* the—I think they said—'the sense of immediacy and place,' which sounds amazing, whatever it means."

"It means I'm an incredible writer and you should always perform my monologues," Libby says, and some girl passes her in school and calls her a mean-girl name and Libby doesn't even respond to her, that's how into this conversation she is. (I don't have the heart to tell Libby I ended up changing parts of her Greyhound monologue. To make it my own.) "It means," she continues, "I'm meant to be your speech-writer when you run for President of New York."

"I can't disagree, Ms. Libby Jones."

"Did you do the scenes again? Did they ask you to read the sides?"

"Yes, only this time I read for E.T.! For E.T. the alien! That's the crazy part. I did all these wacked-out lip trills and blips and blops."

"Like from our animal seminar?" Libby says.

"*Exactly* like that. I channeled the duck you made me play when we were working on lowering my center of gravity. And, in fact, the director told me to pull it *back*, that I was so physically expressive, I'd have to make sure I didn't actually kill anyone."

"Rock star."

"And they asked if I was afraid of enclosed spaces, because the makeup and bodysuit for E.T. is evidently going to be very, very thick, and I laughed and said, 'Enclosed *spaces*? I've practically lived in toilets and lockers for the last three years. I have highly developed, like, cooling-off mechanisms and am perhaps even *more* comfortable being compressed, than not.' And then I lied and said I was going Trick-or-Treating as a Mummy, tonight, for that very reason, and they all howled."

I can almost hear Libby shaking her head in disbelief. "Rock star, Natey. Boss Rock star. So what's next?"

"Well, they just—thanks, Aunt Heidi"—I uncap the Vitamin Water and inhale it—"asked me to wait in the hall while the team talks things over."

"Eeeeek! Hot *Doonesbury*, Nate." (A musical based upon a famed political cartoon your grandparents read; big ol' bomb.)

A clanking school bell rings all the way through

the phone, nailing my eardrum, and Libby says, "Stay with me. I'm going to sit in the front of the school bus with the losers, and keep talking to you."

For the record, Libby always sits at the front of the bus, being, as am I, a loser.

"There's news here, too, Natey-pants."

"Shoot, cowgirl." I'm trying on all sorts of personas today. Wild West Nate! Feels great. Somebody get me a pen: I've even got some ideas for a new autograph.

"James Madison, the boy zero—you with me?" Libby says.

"Yes'm?"

"—tried to plant a stink bomb in the faculty bathroom today, *but* one of his stupid Bills of Rights got the prank wrong. He bought the whole package, allegedly, in West Virginia—"

"Well, there's trouble right there."

When you're from Jankburg, PA, West Virginia is the only thing you can feel even remotely superior to.

"And James lit a *firecracker* instead of a *stink bomb*. Like, a big, pink, bursting-in-the-sky firecracker."

"Holy *Doonesbury*!"

"And turns out Mr. Skinner was in the faculty john dropping a deuce, and the firecracker rolled underneath the stalls and practically burned his ta-ta off."

"No way!"

The casting people come out and walk right over to

Jordan Rylance, and his mother stands up and thrusts her chest so hard into Rex Rollins's face, I think she's actually going to break his nose. I put the phone by my side and watch as Rex shakes Jordan's hand.

And Jordan's face scatters into a sad soup.

"O.M.G.," I whisper to Libby, "I think Jordan Rylance was just released from the audition or something. I think he didn't get any further," and Heidi says, "Nate, be nice," under her breath. But you know what? Heidi's hopping up and down a little.

"I wonder if Jordan'll post *that* on Insta," Libby says. *"Just cut from E.T. on Broadway. Life sucks, but at least I'm still named after a river,"* and we titter. Bad, bad kids. "But hold on," Libby says, "there's more, about the firecracker."

"Burning off Mr. Skinner's hoo-ha?"

I'm waiting for Rex Rollins to come over and cut me. I'm sure it'll happen any moment. If Jordan *Rylance*, who has better teeth than I do and can sing higher, gets cut, why would anyone want *me* around?

"Yeah: Not only did school security launch a firecracker investigation, but there's an even juicier rumor."

"I'm all ears," I say, but then, "hang on just a sec, Libby," and I smile at Rex Rollins as he totally avoids Aunt Heidi and me, walking right past us, back into the audition room. "Jordan," I call out when the door shuts, "everything okay?"

He looks at me and smiles—his tears were those of *joy*—and calls out, "They asked me if I'm afraid of heights!"

The flying-bicycle sequence, of course.

Mrs. Rylance smirks at me and grabs their stuff—the kind of family that travels with *three* rolling suitcases—and wheels him away to the elevator.

"God, this is making me so nervous," Heidi says. "This is why I got out of acting."

"I thought you got out of acting," I say, stunned, "because of annoying ringlet-haired casting assistants."

"Shut up, Nate," Heidi says, and grabs my Vitamin Water back from me to take a final swig. That's a real family-thing to do, to ingest somebody else's backwash. Aunt Heidi's cell phone rings, and she steps away. I go back to Libby.

"What was that, about a rumor?"

"Okay," she says. "So after the firecracker incident, the principal searched James Madison's locker, and he found, like, a raccoon cap and a bunch of stolen answer sheets and other minor-deal stuff."

I would wet my pants trying to steal answer sheets, but I know what Libby means.

"But when school security searched the Bills of *Rights*'s lockers, not only did they find additional firecrackers—like, a buttload of 'em—"

"Yes?" I say, surprised that I am as invested in this

story as I am, given that a group of adults is deciding, four feet away from me behind a wooden door that locks when children storm out of audition readings, if they should ruin my life and send me home. My mom would probably follow Jordan's mom all the way back, on I-78, until his family pulled off into the nice part of town.

Not to be dramatic.

"But you know what else the cops found in their lockers?" Libby says. "Little Bill had a stack of Broadway Playbills. Including *Dreamgirls*."

"Holy moley," I say, or scream.

"So now the rumor is burning through school that little Bill has a secret gay crush on big Bill. James Madison dropped him from his gang and everything. Though *I* think James may have actually planted the Playbills himself. As a distraction from FirecrackerGate. I'm working out the details now." A torrent of children's screams, white noise on Libby's bus journey home, threatens to override key aspects of her story. I practically miss it back there. We'd be eating Clark Bars right now, to line our stomachs for Trick-or-Treating.

"What are you wearing? For Halloween?" I say, maybe avoiding the whole last minute's conversation.

"I think I'm going to go as little Bill," Libby says. "And dress up as a gay dude."

There's kind of a weird silence, and maybe I cough or maybe things just get quiet on her bus, but then Libby says, "I mean, I have absolutely *no* problem with gay people, Nate. Like, the opposite."

"Mm . . . hmm?"

"My favorite step-uncle is gay. And I, like, DVR everything on Bravo."

Uh-huh. "That's cool, Libby."

"I just mean . . . listen, I wasn't trying to kiss you or anything. The other night. In your backyard."

"You—what?" Yes she was. Oh, God, I'd hoped we would sidestep this follow-up forever.

"I know what you were thinking, but I wasn't. Trying to. Kiss you." Her voice sounds like a shaken pop bottle, opened into a geyser. "I could see it freaked you out. But it was, like, a miscommunication."

"I'm not really kissing *anyone* these days, Libby. You know, regardless. I'm not a big kisser." Shut up, Nate. Shut up, Nate.

"All I mean is, I don't have any problem with gay people. That was all I meant."

Aunt Heidi comes back from the window, and I think about Freckles and her, how great they've been with me. "Me neither, Libby. Some of my best friends are gay people."

Rex Rollins and Monica, the spikey-haired dance assistant, come out the door and walk directly over to me, just like that. But something hits me: "Could I just have one more moment?"

Monica laughs. "By all means, bottle dancer."

"Hey, Libby? How's your mom?"

"Aw, Natey. She's good. She's good. I didn't even get to tell you yet: She got in to see some really good doctor at UPMC, next Friday. Got the call this morning and she texted me at school. She feels really optimistic about it. Maybe your dad pulled some strings at the hospital or something."

Well, here goes. "You know what, Libby? He's not—my dad isn't actually a doctor. He's just a janitor at the hospital."

"*Finally*. Nate. I've been waiting for you to just say it. I've always known that. Doctors don't share minivans with their wives."

If Mom and Dad divorce, one of them is going to have to get another car. Oh, God, where will I live?

"That's awesome, Libby, about your mom." Rex Rollins looks at me and kind of gives a WTF shrug. But I flash the "one second" index finger and say, "Libby, don't go as little Bill tonight. Go as a cat. That's what all the girls are wearing in New York. But just . . . don't make fun of little Bill that way. I mean, if it's true, I'm sure he's really embarrassed. About the Playbills."

"You're killing me, kid," Libby says, and then, "Catch me on the flip. I'm pulling up to my bus stop, and I need to put out the spooky fiberglass cemetery stones in the yard. Mom's insisting I decorate the house, to celebrate her good news."

"Bye, Libby." But she's already gone.

There is some small part of me that wants to get home in time to see the Jones's house decked out. To find out more about little Bill's secrets, in the hallways at school. To give Feather a big hug and cry all over his coat.

But a bigger part of me wants this, here. A bigger part of me knows this is my destiny, what thirteen years of torment have prepared me for, like my entire, tense childhood can be unspooled. Set free.

I put my phone away and look up to Rex and Monica. And Heidi reaches out to put her hand on my shoulder.

This is it, Natey.

"Thanks, Nate," they say. And suddenly I see New York as something different: a cruel, real-time video game, where you might get second chances but you only get one life. "We'll be in touch if we need anything else."

That's it. That's all.

They don't even ask if I'm afraid of heights.

Game over.

First Time I Didn't Like a Sweet

It turns out that custard can taste really, really depressing when you're not in the mood for it.

"Nate," Heidi says, "it could mean anything. Honestly. 'We'll be in touch if we need anything else' is open to a lot of interpretations."

"Then why," I say, licking this custard cone as if it's made out of dirty shoelaces or something, "did Jordan Rylance get asked if he's afraid of heights? That's practically *offering* him a part, right there."

I'm following Aunt Heidi into my first subway ride, and suddenly the newness of a musty underground tunnel, of another thing in New York I won't have the opportunity to become bored with . . . well, it makes me so sad that it gets me angry.

"Come here," Aunt Heidi says. "Let's see if they still sell Fun Passes."

We walk up to an awesome electric machine, like

a big video game (even buying mass-transportation tickets here is a ball), and I grunt: "What's so *fun* about today, huh?"

"Aw, come on Nate," Heidi says, literally mussing my hair like I'm *six*, "this was a big day. They made a big deal out of you, and you even got to sing for them again and everything."

"I thought I really had it," I say, staring at this machine ejecting an amazing yellow card, like a credit card, all for me. A ticket to ride the subway, like some rollercoaster to Hades. A rollercoaster back to Jankburg. I bet a rollercoaster back to Jankburg would be completely flat and devoid of thrills, "The first rollercoaster in the world on which you can actually nap," I bet they'd advertise.

"I didn't even read the whole scene," I say. "I obeyed them and everything and just read my part, opposite the reader in the chair. And she wasn't even good as Gertie!"

Aunt Heidi laughs, and we push through the metal bars onto the other side of the station. It takes me about a thousand tries, either swiping too quickly or too slowly, or too stupidly, I bet mostly. I can't even do it. Aunt Heidi has to reach over and swipe me through; I'm so stupid that I can't even manage to swipe myself through a train entrance, and Aunt Heidi can do it *backwards*, not looking. *That's* what it means to be here long enough for it to become home.

"Readers at auditions are generally awful," Heidi says, "that's why they're readers and not real actors." She kind of grimaces and says, "I've been doing so much *work* to be more *positive*. And it's, like, twenty-four hours with *you*, mister"—talking right at me even though I'm staring into the subway tracks, mesmerized at the rats scurrying across the muck—"and I'm right back to my bitter old self."

"It's Jankburg," I say in a drone. "It's the Jankburg in my grey pores, seeping out and ticking you off and getting in the way of your Oprah mind-set."

Aunt Heidi pulls me back, and a tremendous, horrible screeching (the way I probably sounded when I read the E.T. scene) careens down the corner. I reach out and shout, "Aunt Heidi! The rats are going to be killed! They're going to be hurt, at least!" but she can't hear me, such is this screeching. It's so panicked and frightened that, honestly, I can relate to it.

"Why do you hate Jankburg so much, Nate?" Heidi says, finding us a couple of seats. The subway smells *awful*, I will say that.

"It's not that I hate Jankburg. It's that it hates me, Aunt Heidi."

"Oh, who could hate you, Nate?" And if only she knew: the whole student body, led by James Madison, who can't even tell the difference between a firecracker and a stink bomb but has somehow deduced that I'm broken.

"Just *everybody*," I'm about to say, "just everybody hates me," but instead I get lost reading all the subway-car ads.

"So . . . are you ready to see your mom again? Is there anything else we need to talk about?"

"What's to say?" I go, holding my bookbag, resting my chin on top. "It's not even like anyone ever told me what really happened between you guys. Like anyone in this family takes me serious."

Aunt Heidi exhales in such a huge way that I think I see this lady's skirt flip up, sitting across from us—oh my God, that's a *guy*, in a *kilt*—and Heidi says, "You know, your grandma and grandpa were very, very traditional, Nate."

I did know that. They were literally allergic to vanilla ice cream.

"And I just—wasn't *that*. You know? I just wasn't that."

"And Mom was?" I say, even though I know the answer.

"Well, we were just different, Nate. Right from the beginning. She was older than me, and—gosh, we don't have to talk about this."

But she's quiet and can probably hear my brain shouting *Yes we do!* out from behind my bad haircut.

"And," she continues, "you know, I got a tattoo when I was only sixteen. And your mom just . . . in those days especially, *especially* when I got into theater and she was busy going to secretary school and dating your dad, who was quite an athlete before his accident—"

His accident? I never knew about an accident. Dad specifically never talks about the past, and Mom never talks about much, period, in front of Dad. It's all about Anthony. All about Anthony's future and nothing about the past, ever.

"And your mom, she just . . . I felt very *judged* by her, Nate. Especially when I wanted to go off to New York. And right before our parents, before your grandparents, got really serious about their religion, practically cultish actually, I—" She stops and smiles. Plays the opposite. "I found beer in your mom's closet, in her room."

I look away from the subway ads and can tell she's never said this to anyone. Anyone other than her shrink, I bet. I'm the true definition of a shrink: just a shrunken little person with a family full of shattered people.

"And she never forgave me for that. For finding the beer and telling our parents. And they grounded her *so* hard. And they never really made up."

The subway rocks and sways, and finally we break out from underground and, just like that, like a surprise, we're on an outdoor bridge, zooming straight out like a leap. It takes my breath away; for a second I think we're flying, like the driver made a mistake and we're bursting out of Charlie and the Chocolate Factory's glass ceiling.

Aunt Heidi touches my knee and says, "We're Okay, Natey. It's okay."

"Keep going with the story." I'm looking right into the sun. Nobody ever talks about how good it can feel to look right at the sun, probably because it's so dangerous to. But it's a fact: If you look right into the sun, you cannot feel scared or happy or anything. It puts you directly into a neutral state. True.

"You can imagine being your mom, Nate, and getting grounded and having your boyfriend taken away—your dad, now—and how much you'd resent your little sister. Me. And she and I never really made up. We just . . ." Her voice drifts.

You know somebody has really cried a lot of tears over something when they don't cry at the point a normal person would. This story—about sisters not speaking to each other—she should be bawling. But her eyes are bone dry.

That's therapy for you, I guess. Thanks, Aunt Heidi's shrink.

"So—so that's all?" I say. "You told Grandma and Grandpa that Mom had beer and they grounded her and that's why she stopped talking to you?"

"Yes," Heidi says, looking at me and then away, right away. "Yes, that and the fact that I had gay friends once I got to Pitt, and I loved theater, and I didn't want to work at Grandma Flora's flower shop. You know, all of it. We stopped talking because of all of it."

Right. "Of course." A very traditional barn with no room for black sheep.

I get an idea.

"Hey, Aunt Heidi? Do phones work on the subway?"

"Well," she says, shifting and brushing something off her jeans, something that isn't there. "It can be kind of rude to talk on the subway, on the phone—not that everybody *doesn't*—but, yeah, above ground, here, you can use it."

"That's okay," I say. "I just want to text somebody."

I pull out my dying phone (three hours' talk time, *tops*) and compose a text: "hey. in addition to not going as little bill for halloween, can you do me a huge favor & not tell anyone at school about anthony and his beer thing? just keep that to yourself. to us."

And Libby texts back right away: "aye aye, captain manners."

I close my phone and I guess I must be smiling, because Aunt Heidi says, "Good news, Natey?"

"Nah. I'm just trying to not let history repeat itself,

is all," and we pull up to Aunt Heidi's stop and plop down the stairs two at a time, onto the street below.

And for just a second I allow myself to remember that this was an exciting adventure, no matter what, even if I didn't get *E.T.* Even if I have to go home.

James Madison'll be expelled, after all.

And one of the Bills is an outcast now.

Hey. Maybe he'll need a friend.

The Flower's Alive

Freckles meets us at a Duane Reade.

There're Duane Reades in Queens, too, FYI, for people who are thinking of moving out here; though, ask your parents first, because you don't want them showing up at your aunt's house, believe me, if you run away.

Freckles picks up some fruit and milk and deodorant ("I'm low on Arm & Hammer," he says, elbowing me. I must have used a lot.) "Your mom," he says, as some kind of preparation, "is feeling a lot better. I think she's just really embarrassed, and maybe you guys can . . . I don't know. This isn't my family. But maybe you guys can be extra nice to her when you get back."

Aunt Heidi buys fresh flowers for the apartment. I bet you could even get a new *car* at certain Duane Reade locations. And I find a Maxwell House canister (Mom's favorite) and decide to buy her an apology card in the Hallmark section, something that features a cartoon boy crying his eyes out, holding a broken plate. Scenes from my life. At the last minute, I go more mature and buy her a blank card with the Brooklyn Bridge on the cover. Something to help subliminally convince her that the bridges here are fewer but cooler than back home. Maybe she'll let me come back for some audition. Someday.

But I avoid the Reese's Pieces in the candy aisle. Duh.

Freckles asks about the audition. And perhaps my stomach drops and perhaps he can tell.

"Nate," Heidi says, glaring at Freckles, "I'm telling you. You never know what could happen. They just didn't need to see anything else *today*. They could have just said to you, 'Thank you, you aren't going any further at all in the *E.T.* process.'"

For the record, I have heard the phrase "the process" about a jillion times since getting to New York. Still have no idea what it means.

"They could have just cut you. But maybe they're still considering you. You never know."

"That's right," Freckles says, meek.

We pay for everything (Heidi does), and she and Freckles lead me out through the entrance vestibule, and just before we're about to break to the street, I pass another coat-drive box.

"Hey, Freckles, wait," I say, and he turns around. "We wear about the same size jacket, right?"

He laughs.

"For real, though, can I borrow a sweatshirt the rest of the day, back at your apartment? And I'll give it back before Mom and I take off, tomorrow or whatever."

"Okay . . . ," he says.

And I remove the yellow/burgundy thing (it takes a couple tries, it's *that* big) and drop it in the box, shocked at how much work it takes to stuff the whole thing in. Man, was this coat gigantaur. God, there was even a built-in change purse, I see now, and an umbrella holder made of mesh. It kind of had everything going for it but an appropriate fit.

Somebody else'll appreciate it.

"Are you sure your mom would let you donate that jacket?" Freckles says.

"Yeah, it was kind of on loan, anyway."

We race back to their apartment, my bare arms freezing.

Kids are starting to appear in costumes, on the street, looking just like the kids back home. The getups aren't any better, and that really blows my mind; I'd think in New York the ghosts would be ghostier and the witches witchier. But I guess a kid's Halloween costume is the same everywhere. A bunch of little boys, smaller than even me, come toward us, dressed as a pack of cowboys.

"How come y'all don't have horsies," Aunt Heidi says, with a pretty over-the-top drawl, and Freckles sort of nudges her and says, "We have got to address your accent work," and we sort of laugh.

For a second, I think that we're passing a pretty convincing caveman, but it turns out to be a really down-on-his-luck guy, his beard stringy and dotted with bits of food. He is shivering, a ratty tank top hanging from his frame. He reaches out his hand and says, "Spare change, please?"

"Sorry, man," Aunt Heidi says. "We're actors."

We *are*?

We are?

Freckles takes his own coat off and hands it to this man, calling me an inspiration as we walk away.

"Aunt Heidi!" I say. I'm still stuck on being called an actor. To be *part* of this club! It's intoxicating. I guess she's right, though: I've been through a weekend of Broadway auditions, and they didn't even hate me. They even asked to see some of the things I did a second time, even if Garret Charles said, at one point, "I can't figure out why that's so compelling, young man," in his British accent, "but I could watch you slam into that wall a thousand times. It is . . . vibrant, somehow."

Heidi's walking ahead of us, concealing a smirk.

"So *we're* actors?" I say.

Freckles sort of skips, and tickles Heidi, just like a nice boyfriend might, and says, "Are we, Heids?"

And she says, "Oh, we're nothing until something happens. But my old commercial agent called, and they want me to go in for a Talbot's ad tomorrow."

"No way!" I say, or scream. "That's, like, so huge."

"Well," Aunt Heidi says, grinning or trying not to, "it's not huge until I get it. And I don't think people my age even wear Talbot's, so I'm kind of insulted about that. But, yeah. It's whatever. It's nice."

"Wait," Freckles says. "Weren't you going upstate tomorrow? Wasn't Troy taking you on some hayride or something?"

Aunt Heidi sighs, smiling at a girl dressed as a dead girl, and says, "Oh, you know what? I just—I canceled on him."

Freckles hides a smile.

"I said something had come up."

"You're so going to get that Talbot's commercial, Aunt Heidi. You so are." And I know she will, actually.

We get to their lobby, the rain just starting up again.

"Okay, when we get upstairs?"

"Yes?" they both say.

"I don't know what. I don't know what to say to

her, but I need you to stand between us in case she's come to her senses and wants to ground me." Though, hey: I'd technically be grounded in the state of New York.

And just as we're about to get into the elevator, I look over and see that dead lobby plant, from earlier, and—you wouldn't believe it—a single bud, popping up from a branch.

"Look at that," I say, stopping, dropping my book-bag. "Wasn't that thing dead before?"

"It was. Yeah, actually," Heidi says, with real wonderment.

Freckles says, "It's the weirdest thing. We have a joke about that plant. We call it—"

"The Charlie Brown Christmas tree," Aunt Heidi says, completing his sentence. It's a ridiculous thing to call it, of course, because it's obviously a tropical plant and not a tree at all. But I know what they mean by the joke.

I walk over and inspect it and, sure enough, all the leaves have lifted. Raised like they're being held by something small and invisible underneath.

"Elevator's here, Nate," Freckles says. "You should pick off that little flower for your mom."

But I shake my head. "Nah, let's leave it," I say, backing up from the plant slowly. "Aunt Heidi bought flowers. Let's give the little Charlie Brown plant a chance." And the elevator door dings shut and I watch as, I swear to you, the whole plant exhales.

Pushing itself up maybe another half inch.

You have to be as short as Nate Foster to appreciate how big a half inch can feel, or look. Or sound, on a résumé.

We get back to their apartment, but Mom's nowhere in sight. Maybe she just left me here. And, weirdly, I hope she hasn't; I hope she's not back on the road by herself. Dad called me brave. A brave person worries about other people and not just himself.

Heidi pours us all a glass of water, and we sit on the futon, all three of us, and right then the bathroom door opens and out she comes.

Wearing Heidi's Pitt T-shirt.

"Sherrie," Heidi says.

"Heidi," Mom says.

They both stay exactly still, and the way the light is hitting (or maybe it's the fake Halloween lantern in Heidi's window, but still), Mom looks so young. Tired, sure, but so pure, her face scrubbed so clean; her hair up—I didn't even realize it'd gotten this long—in a ponytail. She looks, in fact, just like my aunt, from all those photos Heidi's hiding under the coffee table.

Mom steps forward and shifts on her feet, a baby taking her first walk, and then puts her head in her hands, and her shoulders shake. And Aunt Heidi stands up to walk over, but just stops. Stops and lets out a little cry. The cry of a girl ready to be forgiven, years after having sold her sibling out to a pair of adults who would, a short time later, die on a distant continent.

The cry of a woman ready to weep with her sister.

"I just *stepped* on something," Heidi says.

Or not.

"Like a *mouse* or something."

And that makes Mom and me scream, at exactly the same pitch. And that makes Freckles and Heidi laugh. Thank God.

Heidi reaches down and picks up my lucky rabbit foot, dropped this morning—so early—when Mom flung me across the room. I guess I must have blown that audition all on my own, on account of no rabbit foot.

Aunt Heidi places it back in my hand like it's a rosary.

And when I look up again, the air is knocked out of Heidi's lungs, such is the type of hug Mom is giving her.

And I guess Aunt Heidi *didn't* get rid of all her tears after all, not in therapy or anywhere else.

Because here they are, the Monongahela and the Allegheny meeting Mom's Ohio River, the two of them sobbing like strangers going as long-lost sisters for

Halloween. Trick-or-Treat, and hot *Doonesbury*, they got treat. They ended up with a bag full of treat. And I think one of them keeps chanting "*We have so many missed birthdays to make up for*" but who knows? Their voices overlap in a general emotional girl-babble.

It's pretty embarrassing for Freckles and me, but it's also pretty wonderful for me.

The doorbell ding-dongs, and children squeal outside, and Freckles goes, "Agh! We spent all that time at Duane Reade and didn't even think to pick up candy."

But I say, "One sec." And you better believe it, I've still got a few handfuls of Reese's Pieces in the bottom of my bag.

I open the door, and standing there is a little boy, dressed up as—oh, God—Elliott from *E.T.* A red hooded sweatshirt and everything. It's very meta. He's not just Elliott but actually going as "Halloween Elliott," just like in the movie.

"Nice costume," I say, gulping. Taking him in. Accepting my fate.

And he says, "Who are you supposed to be?"

"Uh . . ."

"He's SuperBoy," Freckles says, coming up behind me. "He's going as SuperBoy, and his costume is underneath."

Freckles sprinkles a raw handful of Pieces (kind

of gross, I know) into the boy's pillowcase, shutting the door.

And if I'm not mistaken—and I'm not—the boy says, quite clearly, "More like SuperFag." With the "Fag" part echoing down the hall and back under the door frame, hovering, infecting everyone in the apartment.

Even when you yourself have gotten used to being harassed, there is still nothing worse than the feeling of your family being mortified for you. You never adapt to that, to that cloak of hot shame.

"That kid's a jerk," Freckles says.

"He's an a-hole, actually," I say. But I really say it, the whole word.

I turn to Freckles and to Mom and to Heidi, to all of them, and say, "He's an a-hole," again. Sometimes there is no greater act of adulthood than swearing in front of your own mother.

But hey. It's like the boy was giving me a preview of life back home. Like he was getting me prepped to return.

And by the way, this isn't one of those things where I tell you that, in life, we're each both a little good and a little bad, all just trying our hardest. That kid's an a-hole, and I'm not. Sometimes people are just a-holes, and you have to decide, every day, which kind of kid you are.

(Not to get all preachy on you.)

Anyway.

I guess this is the part where I pack a snack and get in the minivan. And never look back.

A Boy Soprano with a Gutsy Chest Voice

It wasn't all that bad, you know? I met a cool aunt and her nice roommate, and I might not have seen *Wicked*, or my own reflection without new zits, but it was still an adventure. I'll have escape stories to tell my Flora's Floras coworkers, someday. If my mom even hires me to work there. If I'm lucky enough to fade back into the grey.

("SuperFag," by the way, is still echoing in the hall, lingering so long, the landlord might have to start charging it rent.)

"SuperFag . . . SuperFag . . . SuperFag . . . Su—"

"I'm going to . . . make hot apple cider," Freckles says in about as awkward a way somebody could say anything at all. But he just stands there.

We *all* just stand there.

The apartment is so still, with only the beating of a grandfather clock above my head.

"Well, now what?" I'm about to say, desperate to change the subject. "We need to pick up 'I Heart New York' T-shirts for Libby before hitting the road. That's my only requirement."

But before I can manage any of that, the *tick-tocking* silence is ended by a ringing, from my pocket.

Freckles makes a face at me, the girls still busy Kleenexing their eyes.

Ring ring.

I fish out my phone from the übertight jeans.

Ring ring.

And there it is.

Ring ring.

212.

Ring ring.

Flashing across the screen.

Ring ring.

"It's them!" I yell. "It's *E.T.*!"

Ring ring.

We stare at one another for about a thousand heartbeats (which, here, only lasts a single second) and Freckles and Aunt Heidi both make the same face. Of bewilderment and awe. Of "Oh my God. You *actually* got the show."

Ring ring.

But Mom cuts through all that, clear across the room, walking right up to me. She reaches out her hand—she never does this, other than when seeking repayment after I borrow things from her wallet—and smiles. Mom smiles, at *me*.

Ring ring.

I take her hand, aware that my own is still sweaty with residual Reese's Pieces; that she'll probably get Dad to shout at me later for not being a hygienic-enough child. But no, actually. I don't think she will. She's looking at me in a new way.

Ring ring.

And call me weird (I've been called worse, and always will be), but Mom is rubbing my hand like it's her own lucky rabbit foot. And then Heidi comes up behind her, and she takes Mom's other hand. A hard-won, reunited family of lucky charms.

Ring ring.

"Pick it up, Natey," Mom says, taking a deep breath. Deciding to be different this time. "Pick it up, SuperBoy."

And for a second, it's almost like I don't even have to answer the phone.

Ring ri—"Hello?" But only for a second. "Yes. This is Nate Foster."

Curtain Call

A big round of applause to the folks behind the scenes whose enthusiasm and guidance helped set the stage for *Better Nate Than Ever*—Andy Federle, Anne Zafian, Cheri Steinkellner, Christian Trimmer, Courtney Sanks, Dorothy Gribbin, Justin Chanda, Karen Katz, Katrina Groover, Laurent Linn, Marci Boniferro, Michelle Fadlalla, Michelle Kratz, Mom and Dad, Navah Wolfe, Paul Crichton, Scott M. Fischer, Tom Schumacher, Venessa Carson, and the whole staff at Simon & Schuster Books for Young Readers: Bravo!

And an immediate standing ovation for my agent, Brenda Bowen; and my editor, David Gale. They truly deserve the final bow.

From Page to Screen

A sneak peek at how the book became a movie: Here's Aunt Heidi's introductory scene in screenplay form!

Excerpt from the screenplay for BETTER NATE THAN EVER, written and directed by Tim Federle

---

INT. STEPS ON BROADWAY - CAFE - DAY (D2)

Meet Nate's long-lost **AUNT HEIDI:** a proudly former Midwesterner (thank you very much).

AUNT HEIDI
This is *incredible.* I was *THIS CLOSE* to not coming to this audition today, but something in me was like, *Do it, Heidi*. And then, this. It's like... you're a sign!

Nate is a deer-in-headlights.

NATE
Thank you! I've been called many names in my life, but "sign" is a first!
(then)
Wait, *you're* auditioning for "Lilo and Stitch," too?

Heidi is... wound up. Not used to seeing family.

AUNT HEIDI
Nooo. No, *haha*. I'm two doors down -- did you see all those ladies who are still trying to pass for mid-thirties? We're all up for the same play. It's called "A Solitary Woman." Perfect for it!
(then)
Where is your mother? Is she in the bathroom? All these years of her judging me for following my dreams, being "the black sheep" -- and then she brings YOU to an audition. Ha!
(then)
I love that you're still acting. I'm not surprised. You were the only toddler whose first word was "Me."
(then)
Who's this? Is this your girlfriend?

NATE
No.

LIBBY
We have not chosen a label at this point in our relationship.

Beat. Nate gives Libby a curious look. Heidi catches her breath.

AUNT HEIDI
I'm just so happy to see you.

NATE
(dry)
Mom's not here.

LIBBY
Nate!

NATE
What? It was bound to come out in
like three minutes.

AUNT HEIDI
What do you mean she's not here?
Did your _dad_ bring you?

NATE
Ha. Nooo. He thinks Broadway is a
four-letter word.

AUNT HEIDI
So, wait -- you're telling me --

LIBBY
We ran away from home, lady.

Aunt Heidi gasps. Pulls out her phone.

AUNT HEIDI
(to herself)
Okay. Um. Responsible Adult mode.
(then)
My greatest acting role yet.
(then, practicing)
"Hi, Sherrie, it's your sister, I
know it's been a couple years --
okay, _ten_, I guess -- but FYI I'm
with your son and --"
(then)
Okay, _*why don't I have your mom's cell?*_

NATE
Because it's been a long time since
you've spoken.
(then)
Heidi didn't show up to my parents'
wedding. She was the maid of honor
and everything.

LIBBY
That's... deep.

As Heidi takes a breath to explain further, she's cut off by a PACK OF WOMEN -- all her age, all with her haircut, all on their way OUT -- that exit into the stairwell.

AUNT HEIDI
Aaaand I just missed my audition, so: Awesome.

Nate looks down the hall, at the other kids in line.

NATE
I can't believe you still have to audition.
(in awe)
You've been on Broadway.

AUNT HEIDI
You have _no_ idea, kid.
(then)
What's her number. Spill it. Now.

Libby gives Nate a wide-eyed look. We cut between ECUs on their eyes, like twins sharing a secret language.

NATE
(giving *Libby's* number)
It's. Um. 412-555-8720.

ECU: Libby _*switches her phone to silent*_.

Heidi dials the number on SPEAKER PHONE MODE. Staring at Nate. Jaw clicking. What a day.

Libby's phone buzzes. Nate COUGHS to cover it.

VOICEMAIL (ON SPEAKER PHONE)
You have reached the voicemail box of 412-555-8720. Please leave a message.

BEEEP --

AUNT HEIDI
(into phone)
Hi. Sherrie. Um. I'm with... my nephew. Your son. Nathan.

NATE
Nate.

AUNT HEIDI
Nate. He's alive. I mean, he's twelve seconds from being murdered by his aunt, but he's _*fine*_.
(MORE)

AUNT HEIDI (CONT'D)
I'm going to... Um, I'll get him on the next airplane --

NATE
Bus. We can't afford an airplane.

AUNT HEIDI
-- home. And. Someday we'll all have... a laugh about this? If there's a world where we speak again. Okay. Um. Bye-bye now.

She hangs up. Libby slow-claps.

LIBBY
Incredible work.

AUNT HEIDI
Excuse me?

LIBBY
I truly believed you cared about her. I'm with Nate, I can't believe you still have to audition for things.

Heidi rolls her eyes. From the hallway, we hear:

CASTING DIRECTOR (O.S.)
Okay, first group of kids for LILO! Let's *do this!*

Cheers from the kids in the hall. Heidi regards Nate. He's bouncing up and down a little.

AUNT HEIDI
Alright, let's get outta here --
(then)
Why are you bouncing?

Libby doesn't even look back at Nate. She knows.

LIBBY
This is his pee dance. It's a thing.

NATE
(mock-annoyed)
Libby.

He's stepping on his feet and everything. The works.

AUNT HEIDI
Just go *fast*, okay?

NATE
That's not good for your bladder.

AUNT HEIDI
GO!
(to Libby, as he exits)
Is he always like this?

LIBBY
(smiling)
Hilarious? Yeah.

Here's a sneak peek at
Nate's next big adventure!

Available from
Simon & Schuster Books for Young Readers

The Fun'll Come Out, Tomorrow

In musicals, characters break into song when their emotions get to be too big.

Whereas in *life*, of course, I break into song when my emotions get to be too big. Without getting paid for it, I mean.

"Nate, will you two keep it down *up there? It's almost midnight."*

That's my dad, who has apparently forgotten how exciting my future is about to become. And that people sing and dance in their (incredibly small and poorly decorated) bedrooms when they're excited. Loudly.

"Sorry, Dad!" I shout. But I do this thing where I mouth "I'm not" right before. Gets my best friend laughing, every single time.

"I ought to pack for tomorrow," I say to Libby between huffs and puffs. We have a long-standing Sunday tradition where we belt the entire score of

Godspell until either the neighbors call to complain or I lose my voice. It's our version of church. "I guess I'll need socks? I should pack socks." But this Sunday is different.

"Refocus, Nate," Libby says, dragging me to my own desk. "I've gotta get home soon. And *we* have your first Playbill bio to write."

Cue: hopping, hollering, Dad cranking up "the game" downstairs.

Libby retrieves a stack of beat-up theater programs from her bookbag. "Let's study bios." She has a step-uncle in New York who sends her his Playbills. Can you imagine the luck? This is probably how most normal boys feel when they rip open a pack of baseball cards, suffer through that stick of "gum," and then . . . I dunno. What do boys do with baseball cards? Fan themselves in the stadium heat?

"Flip to the ensemble bios," I say. "We can bypass the stars." We scan the little biographies that actors write about themselves, trying to settle on relevant information I might use to craft my own for *E.T.: The Musical*. "What the heck am I even going to write? I'm allowed fifty whole words to describe a life spent hiding from bullies in bathroom stalls."

"That's a good thing," Libby says, chewing on her lip like she's still hungry. Which you'd know is impossible, if you'd seen the way Libby ate even the *crusts* on our pizza tonight. "Fifty words," she continues, grabbing a pencil sharpener from my *Zorba* mug, "means we get to use a *ton* of adjectives to tell the world where you got your training."

I see where she's going with this. Libby is, among other things, one of the great acting coaches of our time. She's also the only one I know—but come *on*, I'm not even old enough to drive and I'm going to be *on Broadway*. Wowza. Even thinking about it again—

"Nate, you're shaking."

—makes me shake. "I'm just so . . . excited!"

Did you know that "excited" is Latin for "actually-kind-of-nervous-but-in-the-greatest-way-possible"?

"Well *I*, for one, am jealous," Libby says, re-piggying a pigtail. "Not only are you making your Broadway debut—"

(Squealing, jumping, possibly a bedside lamp being broken.)

"—but you *also* get to do your homework online. Not that you participate in class, anyway."

I take this as a compliment.

Knock knock knock, and I practically pee my pants. *"Nathan."* You know when you didn't even know you had to pee until your dad pounds on your door with the kind of strength that's usually reserved for fighting back a burglar?

"Your mother and you are leaving early," he says from

the hallway, and then lopes away. That's all he has to say. Everything is implied with Dad. . . . *so tell that girl to go home* is implied, as is . . . *and stop squealing, because boys don't squeal.*

"You do know you *look* like him," Libby says, "when you make that face—right?"

(. . . *and don't come back home until you've made us some money.* That's also implied. Though I'm not sure I ever *want* to come back. Not unless they name a local street after me. Nate Foster Way. Heck: Nate Foster *Free*way.)

"How about this," Libby says, slipping on a purple Converse. Oh gosh, she really is leaving me soon. "How about you just make it ultracool. The bio? Like, don't even list your junior high theater credits. Just thank people. Important people who have shaped your career. Like . . . peer mentors. Or whatever."

I grin. "Like . . . best friends?"

"Forever," she says, fast.

She kind of wrinkles her nose the way you might see in a cartoon sneeze, fending back unexpected tears. But this is no cartoon. And I'd know, because I've been chased to the edges of cliffs several times after school.

"Who am I going to watch *cartoons* with in New York?"

"We're almost in high school, Nate," she says, switching tones. "We've got to pull it together and quit it with the cartoon business. I've been humoring you, but. Come on." Brilliant move. Nothing averts sobs like insulting somebody.

"Well . . . I should clean out my closet, then, I guess."

Which is technically true but probably won't happen until the very last minute, once my alarm goes off. There's too much to do tonight: get a rough draft of my bio down; brush my dog, Feather, one last time; barf myself to sleep. While thanking the universe in between heaves.

"Yeah," Libby says, opening her bookbag and heading for my bedroom door. "And I should get home. My mom'll worry that I'm here so late."

"Oh?"

"Yeah," she says, smirking. "What if you put the moves on me or something?"

I'm about as dangerous to a girl as a tube of mascara, but maybe that's the joke.

"Your bookbag's open," I say.

"Good eye."

"Are you giving me a going-away present?"

Libby never lets me go on a journey without supplying all the basics that any idiot would remember to bring. Like donuts, primarily.

"No, Nate. I was sort of hoping *you'd* have something to give *me*."

I scrunch my face.

"Something tangible with a hint of your *essence*, Nate. Like . . . a piece of clothing. Or an old Indian-head nickel. Or something."

I laugh. "When did you get so, like, woo-woo?"

"Since none of my mom's chemo treatments took hold," Libby says, skin turning a shade of white that could rival unused towels, "and she started looking into alternative therapies. Is when."

Sting. "Oh. I'm sorry. Wow."

"Yeah. I didn't . . . I haven't had the heart to, like, bring the mood down. Since you've been talking non-stop about *E.T.* for two months."

"Oh God, Libster. I'm really—"

"Not that *I* wouldn't. If I were—you know—*you*."

God, I am such an awful person. An awful friend. And selfish. I look myself over. And fat.

"You are *not* fat," Libby says, reading my mind and dropping her bookbag. "So just stop it. They hired you as you are, Natey. Show up the way they hired you." She swigs from a two-liter of Mountain Dew that I hadn't even realized was in her coat. "You think Meryl Streep would lose weight just to please some costume designer?"

I think Meryl Streep would die if the person she were playing was dead. But I get Libby's point.

"Thank you."

"You're welcome."

"For comparing me to Meryl Streep, I mean."

"Implied."

And at the mere mention of her name, we both burst into Oscar-worthy tears. And sort of fall into each other.

This is it. Good-bye, Jankburg. Hello . . . *everything*.

I hear Dad trudge up the stairs again, but I hold Libby tighter. And before he can *knock knock knock*, I have the guts, boiling beneath seven slices of pizza and a lava of molten Coke, to shout at the top of my everything: "Leave us *alone*, Dad. This is a pivotal moment."

Libby pulls away, her tears stopped quick like a clamped hose, and sniffs back a goob of snot. "Wow," she says. "Where'd that come from?"

"Here," I say, putting her hand on my rumbling stomach.

"Nah," she says, wiping a crystal tear from her porcelain face and placing her hand on my heart. *"Here."*

From outside my room, my father's feet squeak in the carpet as he turns in his thousand-year-old slippers, stomping away to take it all out on my mom.

And I know exactly what to give Libby as a going-away present.

"What was that for?" she says.

"I don't know. I've never . . . had one."

"Well, you could at least have opened your mouth

a little," she says, holding her lips like they're a wounded butterfly.

We both hiccup at the same time.

"If I'd known that was coming, I'd have skipped the last piece of pizza," she says, letting her lips go like they might fly away.

We both can't believe I did that. Kissed someone. Finally.

"I'm . . . I'm going to leave on that note," she says for maybe the millionth time. "Your mom is gonna be pulling the Grand Caravan into the front yard in about five seconds."

But Libby's wrong. I've got longer than five seconds till the next chapter of my life starts—the first one *worth* singing about.

"Yeah."

Heck, I've got five *hours* till my alarm goes off. Maybe I'll even sneak Feather into bed, where he's not allowed for all the obvious mom reasons. Five hours' sleep is five more than Libby and I got on New Year's, and that was only a couple nights ago. Look at us now! Barely yawning.

"I feel like I'm going to fall over," Libby says, her eyes fluttering—like the butterfly forgot which body part it was playing.

"Let's sit on my bed," I say, "and listen to our favorite song." And never say good-bye. "And I'll see you on Zoom tomorrow night, from Queens."

Assuming my aunt has Internet.

"You have the headphone splitter?" I say.

"Was *Sweet Smell of Success* robbed of a choreography nomination?"

Libby pulls out her iPod, but we're practically asleep by the time the song even starts. And maybe it's my murky brain fluid talking, but I get the perfect idea for a going-away gift.

"Gimme your bookbag," I murmur, and Libby does, not even opening her eyes.

I drop it in—the green rabbit foot that hangs by my bed. Libby gave it to me as good luck, forever-and-a-half ago. And carrying it to the audition, that fateful New York day—with that flipping green bunny foot scratching a green bunny nail into my pale Natey thigh—look where all that luck landed me.

My heart speeds up again. This is actually happening. Tomorrow night at this time I'll be avoiding muggers in Times Square.

"There's a surprise in there for you," I say, zipping up Libby's bookbag.

"Good," she says, pulling the earphone from my head, "I was hoping you'd settle on the rabbit foot."

"You peeked?"

"Nah," she says. "Didn't have to."

I guess we both know that the kid with the sick mom could use the rabbit foot more than the kid who's escaping junior high torment.

A light pokes through the slats of my blinds. I sit up straight.

"It's not a burglar, Nate," Libby says, yawning so hard I can hear pepperoni digesting. "The sun's just coming out."

"'Betcher bottom dollar,'" I say. God, I wish there were a boy role in *Annie*.

"Careful, Nate," Libby says, turning a pillow over to find the cool side. "First you kiss me, then you talk about my bottom. People will say we're in love."

"There'd be worse things."

(There'd be worse things than being born a boy who likes girls, believe you me.)

"Broadway's gonna be a piece of cake after middle school," Libby whispers. "You just have to carry our three rules around with you like a loaded water gun."

"You bet."

"One?" Libby says. She's the only thirteen-year-old who gives pop quizzes.

"We text each other so often that our phones break."

"Right. Two?"

"Sing as loud as possible, as often as possible, in as many rehearsals as possible."

"—in order to get more solos. And possibly replace the lead. That's right. And three?"

"I steer clear of Jordan Rylance—*speaking* of leads—at all costs."

"The little *Via Galactica*."

"Watch your mouth," I say, chuckling at our always hilarious routine: substituting Broadway show flops for swearwords. (*Via Galactica* played for, like, four days in 1972, at the Uris Theater. It is only a quasi-flop because it's the same theater where *Wicked* plays, now. So it's automatically sacred, in a way.)

"I'm telling you, Nate, avoid Jordan Rylance. Pretend from day one that he's contagious with something."

Libby knows Jordan—the (luckiest) kid (ever) cast as Elliott in *E.T.*—from before, when she used to go to the fancy performing arts school with him across town. Before her mom got sick. Before Libby had to move to Jankburg, and meet me, and reroute my drifting destiny like a gust of glittery wind.

"What are the odds of two boys from the same hometown getting cast in the same Broadway production?" I say, and I really wonder it. I wonder it deep into my mattress, which I feel like I'm falling into, now.

"What are the odds we'll even fall asleep tonight?" Libby says, or I think she does.

We're too busy falling asleep. One last time.

Legs intertwined. *Wicked* on repeat. Bags not packed.

Before the second adventure of my only lifetime starts—with no lucky rabbit foot in sight.